BOYS LIKE US

Stonewall Inn Editions
Michael Denneny, General Editor

BOYS LIKE US

Peter McGehee

St. Martin's Press
New York

BOYS LIKE US. Copyright © 1991 by Peter McGehee. All rights reserved. Printed in the United States of America. No part of this book may be used or reproduced in any manner whatsoever without written permission except in the case of brief quotations embodied in critical articles or reviews. For information, address St. Martin's Press, 175 Fifth Avenue, New York, N.Y. 10010.

Design by Anne Scatto

Library of Congress Cataloging-in-Publication Data

McGehee, Peter.
    Boys like us / Peter McGehee.
      p. cm.
    ISBN 0-312-06913-8 (pbk.)
    I. Title.
    PS3563.C36374B6   1991
    813'.54—dc20   90-49210
                                       CIP

First Paperback Edition: March 1992

10 9 8 7 6 5 4 3 2 1

FOR DOUG

Acknowledgments

Special thanks to Doug Wilson, Gail van Varseveld, Norman Laurila, Michael Denneny, the Ontario Arts Council, and the Saskatchewan Writers' Colony.

Contents

ILLICIT INVALIDS

I lose people.

Friends, family, lovers.

Sometimes they come back; sometimes not.

Randy answers the door wearing an old brown raincoat. "Can't find my goddamn bathrobe." The walk from the bedroom has exhausted him. "Hope to hell I didn't leave it in the hospital." He eyes my grocery bag. "What's for supper?"

"Fettuccine with bacon and mushrooms—rather, three kinds of mushrooms—just like you ordered."

He plops down on the couch. "I've got the most horrible taste in my mouth."

"Want a beer?" I go to the kitchen and open one for myself. "You can still drink beer, can't you?"

"I can drink anything I want to drink," he says, irritably flicking on the television by remote control. "But all I want's a Perrier."

I roll my eyes and pour him a glass.

Good thing he's such an old friend or I just might not put up with him. We've known each other fifteen years. I met Randy in New York, at the intermission of a Broadway show. He took me for drinks afterwards, down to some bar in the Village. That's where our wild affair began. And it lasted exactly five days.

"Here you go, sister." I hand him his drink, the fizz of it sprinkling my wrist.

"Thank you," he says in a surprisingly pleasant tone.

On my way back to the kitchen, I turn off the television manually.

"Hey!" he protests.

"Talk to me," I say.

"About what?"

"Anything." I watch him through the pass-through and start chopping garlic. Lots of garlic. "What's the matter? You tired?"

He makes a face. Stupid question. "Of course I'm tired." He folds his arms over his chest, shuts his eyes, and drifts off.

I make certain the pasta's not too soft, the bacon not too greasy, and the mushrooms just this side of crisp. I fix his plate like the best of chefs.

"Do you want this on the couch or at the table?" I ask, nudging him awake.

"What?" he mumbles, groggy, slow to come to.

"Your dinner," I reply.

He looks at the plate, then at me. "It smells terrible."

"It's exactly what you asked me to fix."

"Well, I don't want any."

"You've gotta eat, Randy."

"I know I've gotta eat!"

He sits up. His raincoat comes undone. His genitals flop out. They look huge, the only part of him that hasn't lost a quarter of its weight.

"Do you know what these mushrooms cost?" I ask.

"Of course I know what they cost! I buy them all the time."

"OK. Fine. You wanta starve? Starve."

"You're a terrible nurse."

"And you think you're some hayride?"

I almost get a grin out of him.

He looks around the room, looks anywhere but at me. "I met a social worker in the hospital," he says, "who told me what to do when I get to the point of no return."

"Cheery subject."

"You have to be prepared for these things, Zero. Start stashing pills—"

"That's a great attitude, Randy."

"I'm just saying why would I deny myself the humanity I'd grant a dog?"

"Why don't I get out my date book and we'll set an appointment to go pick out your coffin?"

"I won't be needing a coffin. I'm gonna be cremated. I've already written out my funeral instructions. They're in my top dresser drawer. Just so you know." He picks up his plate. "I'll have that beer now, if you don't mind."

"I don't mind." I get it for him.

He eats voraciously.

After he's finished, he pushes himself up from the couch and walks out on the balcony. His apartment is on the twenty-eighth floor. It's a warm June night. There's a slight breeze, and the air's so clear you can actually see the horizon.

We stand there together, taking it all in. I look at him, trying to see beyond the anger and bitchiness and figure out what the hell I can do to help him.

"Stop looking at me like that."

"Like what?"

"Like I'm already gone."

He walks back into the apartment, pulling the raincoat tightly around him.

"As soon as I gain some weight back. As soon as I get on AZT. As soon as I get on everything else they've got in store for me, things'll be just fine."

"It's good to hear you say something positive."

"Yeah, I'm real positive," he says sarcastically, "a real positive kind of guy. Why, Zero? Why now? If it had to happen, why couldn't it have just waited one year? I've got more work lined up for next season than I've ever had. Not to mention my first big movie. If I have to drop out of that—"

"You won't. You've got all summer to rest up for it."

"Yeah, I've got all summer." He walks toward the window. "I made you the executor of my will."

"I'm gettin' another beer. You want one?"

"I'm leaving most everything to you. Except for my body. And that goes to the hunkiest necrophiliac you can find!"

He cackles until he chokes. I just stand there and wait for his breathing to return to a healthy wheeze. Then I suggest he go back to bed. For once, he doesn't argue. Slowly, we tackle the hall.

I sit with him until he falls asleep, then clean the kitchen and leave a note for Searcy, who's coming to do breakfast.

I look in on him once more before I go. He's half awake, sweaty, and, when he sees me, he holds out his hand. It floats toward me like something exempt from gravity. I touch it. Grab hold.

As our fingers intertwine, he asks, "Does that feel like me or like somebody else?"

"It's you, Randy. It's you," I assure him. "Are you sure you don't want me to stay the night?"

"I'm sure. You think I'm scared, but I'm not."

I kiss him on the forehead. "I think you need some rest."

I walk down the hallway and let myself out.

Riding down in the elevator, I speak cordially to his neighbors, who have no idea about this thing that has so violently shaken our lives.

Walking home, I think about everything.

Everything, that is, but him.

Clay sits on the couch reading a new *Maclean's*. He's still in his Bay Street clothes, but he's loosened his tie and kicked off his shoes. That's the first thing I see: his feet.

"How's Randy?" he asks without looking up.

"The same."

"And what about you?"

"I'm OK."

"Your mother just called."

"What'd she want?"

"Just to see if she had your new number right. I love that Arkansas accent of hers. You can positively swim in it!"

"Fine for you, but I'll do my swimming in a nice cold gin and tonic." I move to the bar and start plopping ice cubes in a glass. "Want anything?"

"Not till after the gym."

"You haven't been yet?"

"Do I look like I've been? Don't you see this body deteriorating before your very eyes?"

"Give me a break, Clay. You've got about the best body I've ever seen."

I walk past him to the bedroom.

I open his closet instead of mine. I love to stare at Clay's clothes. Sometimes, when he's not home, I spend hours at it. Everything's so neat. The row of suits, slacks, and freshly laundered shirts. The stacks of T-shirts, chinos, and jeans. The cotton sweaters so carefully separated from the wool—

"What are you doing?" he asks incredulously, standing in the doorway.

"Uh, looking for my tennis shoes," I say quickly, shutting the closet doors. "You haven't seen them, have you?"

"Well, they wouldn't be in there." He laughs.

"They wouldn't?"

"No."

He comes toward me. Gives me a kiss. His tongue, thick and salty. And I lose myself. Let him carry me away.

I stand in front of the toilet pulling the condom off my cock. I toss it in and flush. Watch it swirl in the water, then disappear. I imagine my sperm surviving the sewers of Toronto, working their way into Lake Ontario, and impregnating some carp. Is any sex safe?

Clay lies like an unwrapped package in the remains of

his shirt, trousers, and belt. Cum dots his belly. I write in it. The word *love*.

"Say it," he says.

"I just did."

"Out loud."

"No."

"Why not?"

"I just don't want to."

"What's so hard about it? 'I love you.' See? It's easy."

My eyes unexpectedly fill with tears.

"Come on," Clay says, trying to hug me. "It's OK," he says, thinking it's Randy, but it's not. It's him. Three months we've been together, and I still don't know what to make of us or me or anything, for that matter.

"Go to the gym," I tell him. "Just go."

I work through the list of people still to be called about Randy. They all ask, "So how is he?" What they really mean is, How long? I begin with the best scenario: how much better treatments are now as opposed to five years ago. . . . Usually they don't ask, "What if?"

I manage to set up a shopping and cooking schedule for the next two weeks. I also manage to drink a quarter bottle of gin.

Clay comes home sweaty and ripe. He thinks this excites me. And it does. Sort of.

He steals my drink. Walks out on the balcony. When I finish the conversation I'm in the middle of, I join him.

The moon, like a big bruised plate, shines through the girders of an unfinished office tower. A string of planes speckle the horizon on their final approach to the airport.

"Nice view," I say, gripping the rail, twisting my hands around it like a gymnast would a high bar. "Ever wonder what it'd be like if it was you?"

"If what was me?" he asks.

"Who got sick."

"Sure, but it's not gonna be. And it's not gonna be you either."

"How do you know? Look how long it took to show up in Randy."

"I just know." He smiles. He is so sure.

I pat the sleazy nylon of his gym shorts.

We go to bed. I don't sleep well. It's like my adrenaline's gone berserk. Just as I'm about to drift off I feel it speed beneath my skin like a thousand different screams. What would they say if they had words?

The next morning at work, I sip a cup of black coffee and stare at my in-basket. I'm convinced it comes alive at night. Like in a Disney cartoon, the jobs multiply. Rearrange themselves. Become even more boring than they ever really were. Corrections. Changes to layout. . . .

"Zero"—buzzes the receptionist—"you've got a call on line two."

"Thanks."

I pick up on an irate Randy.

"Who the hell put Searcy on the breakfast shift?" he demands to know.

"Why? What'd he do?"

"Spent an hour and a half ranting at me about diet, psycho-healing, and a million other cockamamie theories. Like spiritual whistling. Have you ever *heard* of spiritual whistling?"

"He's just trying to be helpful."

"Well, I am hardly in need of advice from an overweight drag queen!"

"He's a female impersonator, Randy. Will you ever get that straight?"

"Just take him off the list!"

"All right! God! You'd think I had nothing else to do all day but cater to your every whim."

"You don't," he says, suddenly jovial. "Now who's coming for dinner?"

"Me."

Maurice, my boss, appears at my desk.

"Gotta go," I say to Randy.

"Why?"

"I just do." I hang up.

"Personal call?" asks Maurice.

"Family business," I tell him.

He hands me a fresh pile of chaos. "A few more things I'd like you to look at. But first, can I see you in my office?"

" 'May I,' Maurice. How many times do I have to tell you? It's 'may I,' not 'can I.' As the editor of a magazine, you really ought to know the simple rules of usage." I follow him in.

He sits down at his desk. Folds his hands in front of him. "Was it really necessary for you to break into song during yesterday's board meeting?"

"I can't see that it really mattered. No one was listening to anybody anyway. I was only trying to prove that point."

"You are not there to *prove* anything. You're there to take notes."

"I am not supposed to be there, period. It's your job to go to board meetings, not mine."

"Your job is to do what I can't get to."

"That's not what I was told when I was hired."

"This is a small operation. We all have to pitch in."

"You're lucky I'm talented."

"You're lucky you are too. Now, I've got a new girl coming in next week. Once you train her on the typesetting program—"

"I am not training anyone on that program."

"Oh, yes, you are."

"No, I'm not." I start to walk out.

"Zero!" he yells.

"Forget it!" I shut the door behind me.

I fume my way over to Snookums' drafting table. He's working furiously on a drawing. His whole body shakes to the motion of his pencil, slowly dislodging his notorious hairpiece.

"Back from the war zone?" he queries.

"Am I showing any wounds?"

"Nary a scratch."

"I hate this, Snookums. Maybe I should've stuck to free-lancing. I wonder why it suddenly bothered me that I didn't have a stable job?"

"Age. Don't worry. Maurice will lay off eventually. He's just testing you."

On another subject altogether I ask, "Have you, by any chance, talked to David lately?"

"Yes, precious."

"Did you tell him I wanted to see him?"

"Yes, precious."

"And?"

"Nothing, precious."

I emit an exasperated sigh. "Eight years together, and we can't even have a friendly divorce. We're making a lot of progress in this life, aren't we, Snookums?"

"The general level of stupidity has always astounded me. But your David does not belong in that category."

"He is not my David."

"Was for eight years."

"And those eight years are over."

The receptionist buzzes me with another call. I take it on Snookums' extension. It's Clay and there's a faint lisp to his voice, which means he's excited about something.

"What's goin' on?" I ask.

"About thirteen million in Hong Kong. How 'bout you?"

"Oh, the usual nightmare."

"Listen, I just found out I have to go to Montreal to-morrow. They want me to check on our branch office. I thought I'd better let you know in case we had any plans that conflicts with."

"None I can think of. But if you've gotta go out of town, why don't you take me to dinner tonight?"

"Where do you want to go?"

"Downstairs at Fenton's? We haven't been there in a while."

"OK. I'll have my secretary call for a reservation."

"But make it for eight o'clock. I need to go by Randy's first."

"Good. That'll leave me just enough time for the gym."

"Just see you don't wear yourself out."

"Don't worry."

"Later."

" 'Bye."

I hang up.

"Well!" says Snookums. "Aren't we Miss Assertiveness Training!"

"Not to worry. It's just my latest act." I straighten his hairpiece with one deft flick of my wrist.

At lunch, I run into Searcy. He's coming out of his aerobics class as I'm walking up Church Street. He hollers my name in that affected lilt of his. (Guess what the biggest influence on his tortured youth was? *Brigadoon*.) "Got time for a cup of coffee?"

"Sure."

He waltzes me into Brandt's, pulls a couple of stools up to the sandwich bar so we can look out the window, then gets us each a cup. He dumps two packs of sugar into his. "Exercise is killing me," he says. "I also think it's making me gain weight!" He drops his stir stick dramatically. "I suppose you've spoken to Miss Randall?"

"As a matter of fact, I have."

"Why does he hate me so?"

"He doesn't hate you, Searcy."

"He does too! With the exception of the one and only

night we spent together, he's been nothing but a certifiable bitch."

"I didn't know you spent a night together."

"Oh, yes! About a hundred and ten years ago when we were children and didn't know any better. He used to cherish my advice. Used to worship the ground I made thunder. But you tell me what to make of him now!"

"He just needs a little time to deal with this in his own way."

"But honey, I've been seropositive since the antibody test was invented, and have you ever seen a brighter picture of health? Can I help it if I happen to advocate certain therapies? I mean if he wants to live—"

"He wants to live."

"Well, I was only trying to tell him that a strict macrobiotic diet—excusing the odd cup of coffee and cocktail, of course—is the key to longevity."

"Be patient with him, Searce. I'd say he's probably still in shock. I know I am. No matter how many people I see get this thing, no matter how many people I know, I still can't believe it's really happening."

"That's what we call denial. DE-NI-AL. DO-RE-MI."

I change the subject. "How're things goin' down at Show Babies?"

"Honey, these lips are still synching shits. But wait till you see our new show. We open three weeks from Friday. Be there or die!"

"Don't worry, I'll be there. Who're you doing?"

"Ethel, Roz, Angela—all the Broadway favorites. But that's nothing compared to this new Barbra Streisand we've got coming up from the States. Perfection in a nutshell. Or should I say with nuts?"

"With nuts is probably more appropriate."

"I prefer cashews. How about you?"

"Pistachios."

Searcy glances at his Lady Timex. "Shit bricks! I'm late for a fucking fitting!" He jumps up off his stool. "I never should've studied method acting. I take it all much too seriously." He throws his dance bag over his shoulder. "Toodles, hon. And you tell Miss Randall to take care of himself."

"I will."

The actress exits.

I order a ham sandwich to go and take it with me back to work. The office is blessedly empty. I eat at my desk.

I dial David's number on the speakerphone. I listen to it ring a few times. I listen to him say hello. "Hello," he says, a second time. Then, more forcefully, "Hello? Hello! *Hello!*" I punch the release button, pick up a bottle of White-Out, and spend the next half hour updating my address book.

I complain to Randy about Maurice.

"You never should've taken that job," he says. "You never should've given up on your own work. It serves you right."

"You're so sympathetic."

"I'm sick of hearing about it."

"Well, excuse me!"

"If you hate it so much, why don't you just quit?"

"And do what? Go back to square one?"

"How should I know? I have enough trouble trying to live my own life without having to live yours too."

"Well, what's up your ass, Miss Thing? I hope you haven't lost another dildo."

"Nothing is up my ass, Zero. I'm just cooped up in this apartment all day trying not to think about anything. Try it sometime. It's a lot of fun."

"Maybe it'd help if you did."

"Oh, yeah? And just what's there to think? You live, you die. It's very very simple. What's for supper?"

I throw up my hands. "Whatever you want."

"You mean you haven't gotten it yet?"

"I just got off work!"

"Great," he says sarcastically, then flicks on the TV. Flicks through the channels. Flick-flick-flick-flick-flick.

"Will you please stop that?" I ask.

"What?"

"Acting like you're the only person in the world this is happening to."

He flicks through the *Wheel of Fortune*. Flicks through several versions of the news, then stops on a *That Girl* rerun, seemingly engrossed as Marlo whines to Don about Daddy.

"Do you really watch this show?" I ask in amazement.

"I fucking love it," he says.

"Since when?"

"I never fucking miss it! If you knew me at all you'd know that much."

I'm late getting to the restaurant. I see Clay before the maître d' sees me, so I seat myself.

Clay hands me a half-finished martini which I down in one gulp. The gin immediately begins its soothing slow crawl through my brain.

"I'll need another one," I say. "Fast."

"Already ordered." Clay smiles. "Randy was in rare form, I take it?"

"Rare form indeed. If he wasn't sick I think I'd kill him."

Clay's smile turns carnivorous.

I slip my foot out of my shoe. Let it graze up his leg. Feel the contour of his calf. His knee. His inner thigh.

"You're gonna get yourself into trouble," he warns.

"Don't worry," I quip. "The tablecloths go all the way to the floor."

He pulls my foot to his crotch. I feel his erection through his pants. As we proceed to read the menu he somehow manages to unzip his fly and pull off my sock so that we're skin to skin.

"What if they had a fire drill right now?"

"We'd probably get a free dinner."

A waiter finally arrives to take our order.

"The broiled artichoke leaf," says Clay, "and the potato skin shish kebab to start. Then he'll have the chicken wing and I'll have the blackened fishtail."

"What?" says the waiter. "That's not on this month's menu!"

I die laughing.

"Two salmon specials," Clay tells him. "And what about those martinis I ordered?"

"That's the cocktail waiter's department," he snaps.

"Well, if you see him, let him know we still exist."

Clay comes about the same time the salads do. The look on his face is unmistakable.

"Are you all right?" asks the waiter, dousing the greens with vinaigrette.

"Allergies," Clay tells him. "Perhaps you could bring me a few Kleenex."

Snookums, a reformed alcoholic, takes me up to Robert's after work for a drink. "I'll just have a spritzer," he says. "They don't really count as booze."

I say nothing.

"Guess who I saw last night?"

"Who?"

"David."

"And—"

"He actually asked about you."

"I don't believe it."

"It's true! Wondered how you were, how you were getting along."

"And what'd you tell him?"

"That the only mistake you ever made was breaking his heart."

"I did not break his heart, Snookums. You know as well as I do, David and I had been talking about living separately for two years."

"But you didn't actually move until you met someone else."

"So what? Never get involved with someone who's perfect. You can never win."

"I mean it, Zero."

"I do too. Where David's concerned, I'm eternally guilty."

Snookums drains his glass. "You wouldn't tell if I had one more, would you?"

I register a friendly warning but just say, "I'm not gonna police you."

"Precious thing." He pats my cheek, then motions to the bartender.

He takes a big sip off the fresh drink, sighs heavily, and says, "Did you know David's decided not to join us for Christmas? We're already in the process of booking, if you can believe it. We never should've told anyone about our Caribbean hideaway. It's getting harder and harder to get a decent bungalow each year."

"Why isn't David going?"

"Says it'll remind him too much of you. He's doing Key West instead."

"Poor thing. He must be seeing someone."

"All I know is he's about ready to see you."

"What?"

"That's the message."

"You're kidding."

"No." Snookums smiles, draining the second spritzer and motioning for a third.

"Two I can ignore," I tell him, "but not three."

"There's nothing wrong with three little spritzers, precious."

I fix him with a cold stare.

"Christ!" he exclaims. "Never spend a minute in a detox

center. Your friends just won't leave you alone after you do."

"At least your friends are speaking to you."

"Well," he grumps, "it's no fun sitting in a bar with an empty glass. Come on, and I'll walk you down to David's."

"Now?"

"What's wrong with now?"

I walk up the steps to David's house and knock on the door. I feel like I did as a child when my mother would make me go apologize to someone my semiretarded cousin and I had bombed with a water balloon.

David doesn't help matters much. He answers the door like a dog that's been hit with too many newspapers. I try to hug him, but it's hopeless. "Good to see you," I say, force of habit.

"You too." He speaks through frozen lips. "Have a seat."

"Thanks." I settle in one of the armchairs and start fishing around in my backpack, the leather one he gave me on our fifth anniversary, for my inventory list.

"How have you been?" he asks.

"I've been great."

"And Clay?"

"Let's leave Clay out of this, OK?"

"Fine. But it seems silly to avoid mentioning him. He *is* a pretty big factor in our lives now."

"*My* life, David."

"May I get you a beer?"

"I'd love one."

He clips into the kitchen. I take a good look at the cluttered living room. It definitely lacks my touch.

He hands me the beer. "So what did you want to see me about?"

"You mean you don't know?"

"Is this gonna be another one of your guessing games?"

"My stuff, David! You've only been holding it hostage since the day I left."

"And just what, pray tell, do you consider yours?"

I hand him my list, adding, "All I really care about's my records, my books, and half the paintings."

"Half?"

"I think I'm entitled to half. We did collect them together."

"Which half?"

"I'll pick one, then you pick one. That's the only fair way. But just remember, I'm leaving you the TV, the rug, and all our furniture."

"Which gives you the right to loot my home?"

"Our home. I've been pretty patient about this."

"Patient!"

"Oh, quit pretending like it was all some big surprise. Like for no good reason I just up and bounded out of here. There're things you never understood about us, David, and you never will. You act like we hadn't a problem in the world."

"There're always problems."

"I'm not being unreasonable."

"Oh, no, you never are."

"I just want what's mine."

"I think we should wait and discuss this at a time when we can do it without becoming so emotional."

"Who's emotional? This is not emotion! This is frustration!"

He smiles, pleased to have whipped me into a frenzy. "How's work?" he asks in a completely different tone.

"Horrible. As horrible as you."

"Is that why you call me every day during your lunch hour?"

"I don't call you."

"Sure you do. You dial my number, listen to me say hello a few times; then you hang up."

"I do not!"

He grins. "Actually, I'm beginning to like the idea of life after Zero, pun intended, and I'm quite prepared to release some of your paraphernalia."

"So you *have* been seeing someone."

"Perhaps I have."

"Move me out and him in, is that it?"

"What do you care?"

"I care a lot. I sincerely want you to be happy."

"And I sincerely want something terrible to happen to you."

"Don't you think it's about time you took those pins out of the voodoo doll?"

"Don't give me any ideas."

"When are you gonna realize I only did what I thought was best, that I only did what I had to do. It seems to me after eight years together we could at least be friends."

He roars with laughter.

"What's so funny?"

"I beg your pardon. But you just don't seem that much better off to me."

"How would you even know?"

"Just tell me what happens when this Clay thing blows over. Is that when you come crawling back on your hands and knees? Well, I'm telling you here and now you won't get past the front door."

"What makes you so sure it will blow over?"

"Come off it, Zero. He's even more self-centered than you."

"I'm amazed at how bitter you are. I really am. In fact, it'd be kind of flattering if it wasn't such a pain in the ass." I get up to leave.

"You can come for your stuff on Friday," he says bluntly. "Friday after work. I'll help you load it in a taxi."

We look at each other with the same awkwardness as when I arrived.

Thursday night Randy wants me to go with him to Boots. "The patio's open," he says, "it won't be too smoky, and we can boy-watch."

"Yeah, a bunch of suntanned twenty-year-olds with blow-dried hair and too much cologne. My favorite dish."

"You've just been out of circulation too long, Zero. You go from one lover to the next and miss out on whole generations."

"Thank god."

"Pick me up about nine?"

"Yeah, sure."

When I get to Randy's apartment, he's sitting in the middle of the living room floor surrounded by stacks of old pictures and papers. This is his latest kick: clearing things out. His wastebaskets are always full, and it bugs the hell out of me.

"I thought you said you'd be ready."

"I am ready."

"Then let's go."

We walk the few blocks up to the bar. Right away we run into a couple of Clay's friends, Jim and Jon. They've been together fifteen years and look exactly alike. They have the same facial hair, the same checkered shirt, the same size 501s bleached exactly the same at the crotch.

"Fancy meeting *you* here!" one of them exclaims, in a voice full of innuendo.

"Out carousing while Clay's in Montreal?" asks the other.

"We were just talking to Clay last night!"

"Oh? And how was he?" I ask.

"Sounded fine."

They smile effusively, like the Scientology people who try to lure you off the street to take an IQ test.

"But we talked more to Paul than to Clay."

"Paul is Clay's ex."

"He was hosting his annual solstice party."

"First year we've missed it."

"Ex?" I say before I can stop myself.

"Ancient history," assures Jim.

"University days," adds Jon.

"We all went to Europe together," one explains.

"After graduation."

"Clay's staying over at Paul's if you should need to get ahold of him."

That knocks the wind out of me. "Thanks," I say icily, trying not to let it show. "But I have the number he gave me at his hotel."

"Well," they twitter, "guess it's time to get our little bums out on the dance floor. Good to see you, Zero. We'll all have to get together for a smart something sometime soon!"

I force a smile onto my face and watch them disappear into the crowd. I feel Randy's delight at my jealousy. "Don't say a word," I tell him.

"Wasn't about to."

Vigorously, I peel the label off my beer.

Walking home, Randy tries to comfort me. "Exes aren't threatening, Zero. If they were, they wouldn't be exes."

"I know. It's my own damn fault. It's not like we've sworn a vow of monogamy. It's just that I'm always saying I'm not gonna get too involved, I'm not gonna go overboard. Then there I am: trapped again. Isn't it possible to love someone without going crazy?"

"You're such a sweet little fool, Zero."

"Why? What have I done now?"

"You let yourself get so wrapped up over the strangest things."

"There's nothing strange about feeling bad when your boyfriend's screwing around with his ex and lies to you about it. I don't care how modern you are."

"Just look me in the eye and tell me I don't mean more to you than Clay or David or all the rest of 'em put together."

I stand there, stunned. It's true, of course. What's shocked me is that he's said it.

Then he kisses me, European style, on both cheeks. "Think about it," he says, crossing the street toward his building. "Just think about it."

The first thing I do when I get home is pick up the phone and call Clay's hotel. Yes, he's registered; but no, he's not in.

I sit on the couch and fume. I try to read but cannot concentrate. I go to bed but cannot sleep. I get up to make sure the door's locked. Then I check to see if the oven's off, even though I haven't used it all week.

Again, I call the hotel. No answer.

I sit on the couch and flick on the television.

The Love Connection is on, that sick late-night game show where they arrange blind dates on the condition that the contestants come back two weeks later to tell the studio audience how much they hated or loved each other.

I call the hotel again.

I'm not comfortable in Clay's apartment, I decide. It's his, not mine.

I call once more. Let it ring and ring and ring.

Forget it.

I grab a stack of paper off Clay's desk, then take a seat at the dining room table and cover the entire surface with blank pages.

I test six different pens, but none of them will do.

I write nothing.

I throw the pens across the room.

Nothing satisfies me. Nothing.

Randy drops by Saturday morning to inspect the loot I've brought from David's. "Did you get the paintings?"

"Half."

"Well, what are we waiting for? Let's hang 'em."

"Don't you think I ought to consult Clay first?"

"Why? Did he consult you before settling on this design scheme? Besides, who could argue with your little jewels over a bunch of dry-mounted train posters?"

"Clay likes train posters."

"Surely we could get away with a few."

I look at the pile of my worldly possessions and suddenly wonder why getting them back was so important.

"Life's sad," I say, "and we're sad right along with it."

"Oh, all you need's side two of *Hello, Dolly!* That'll pull you out of your funk." Randy stretches out on the couch. "I'll just instruct from here, if you don't mind. Got a hammer?"

By the time we finish, the room is completely rearranged. Furniture as well as pictures.

Clay has a fit.

"We can change it all back," I tell him. "But why don't we just live with it a few days?"

"I don't believe this!"

"Look, we just hung one, then another. We got a little carried away, OK?"

"No, it is not OK. This room has been exactly the same since I moved in."

"No kidding."

"I'm going to the gym, and when I get back I expect to find my home the way it was."

"Yeah? And just where do I fit into this floor plan?"

"You fit."

"Sure. You want me to move in; then, when I do, you turn on me."

"I said, you fit!"

Pause.

"How was Montreal?"

"Busy and boring and thank you for asking."

"I tried to call you the other night."

"I didn't get a message."

"I didn't leave one. I figured if you weren't in by four in the morning you probably weren't gonna be."

"I'm sorry. I must've been at Paul's. I should've called you."

"No need. I ran into Jim and Jon. They told me all about

it. Nice and cozy with your ex. I didn't even know you had a Montreal ex."

"Paul's been very upset," he says quietly.

"How sweet you were there to comfort him, not to mention attend his annual solstice party."

"His lover's in the hospital with pneumocystis."

"Shit, Clay—"

"Just put the room back."

I do not put the room back. I change it even more. When Clay comes home he doesn't say a word; he just carries me off to bed.

Afterwards, I have to ask him, "How're we gonna solve our differences once sex wears off?"

"It won't. Not if I have anything to do with it."

"Well, having just come from an eight-year relationship, I hate to tell you, but it does. Believe me."

"So? We don't have differences. Not really."

"What we don't have is similarities, Clay."

"Where they matter we do."

"Yeah? And just where's that?"

He climbs on top of me.

"Stop," I tell him.

"I want you to feel something."

"I've felt it."

"Something else." He lies on top of me. Very still.

"Feel it?" he asks.

"What I feel is your heart pounding."

"Yes. Only inches away from yours and just slightly out of sync."

■ dump Randy's AZT capsules out on the table and arrange them into a five-pointed star.

"What are you doing?" he asks.

"Voodoo. I learned it from David. When'd you take your first dose?"

"Seven this morning."

"How do you feel?"

He reaches for the remote control. "I wish everyone would stop asking me that." He turns on *That Girl*. Marlo and Don are devising a Mardi Gras costume. They're going as a worm. She's the front half and he's the back.

"You only watch this show because it's the worst sitcom in the history of television."

"I watch this show to stay in touch with how bad good TV acting can be. Besides, when I lived in New York I used to cater for Marlo."

I try to watch it with him, but the laugh track is so nauseating I finally have to go out on the balcony for some fresh air. I lean over the rail and wonder what it'd be like to jump.

At the next commercial break he joins me.

"What's wrong?" he asks.

"I told you, I hate that show. I don't see why you can't tape it and watch it when I'm not here."

"OK. What else?"

"You were right about what you said the other night."

"What?"

"That I loved you. More than Clay. Or David. Or anybody, for that matter. And you're such a stupid asshole for waiting till now to realize it."

He starts to say something, but his voice trails off. The only thing I catch is, "I hope—"

JESUS
LAS VEGAS

Randy is taking all the latest medicines in all the latest dosages and enjoying what his doctor cynically refers to as "the honeymoon period." I prefer to say: Life goes on. And indeed it does.

Begrudgingly, Randy agrees to accompany me to Searcy's opening, though he piddles around his apartment long enough to make sure we're good and late.

The new Barbra Streisand is doing "The Music That Makes Me Dance" from the stage version of *Funny Girl* when we take our seats. The image is flawless, the acting style even more so.

He's followed by a chorus number, a solo spot featuring Julie Andrews in *My Fair Lady*, then Searcy as Bette Midler wrapping up the first act with "The Rose." That's his signature song. It's very touching. You can actually hear him singing on top of the tape, slightly off key and just a beat behind.

The minute the lights go up on intermission, a beehive of activity ensues. Boys, boys, and more boys. Looking around, being around.

Intermission at Show Babies is at least forty-five minutes. You know, give the folks plenty of time to knock back the booze.

Randy and I cruise the crowd from our table. I notice a young man leaning against the bar. He's wearing jeans and a T-shirt and has a short haircut.

He smiles. I smile back.

Lo and behold, it's the new Barbra Streisand!

"S'cuse me," I say to Randy, getting up.

I make my way over to the bar.

"That was quite a performance," I say. "And you're the one face in this crowd I thought I hadn't seen."

"The art of the illusion," he observes wryly, in a heavy Southern twang.

"Where're you from?" I immediately ask.

"Arkansas," he tells me.

I just about fly out of my shoes. "Really? So am I!"

"No kidding! What part?"

"Little Rock. And you?"

"Oh"—he shrugs—"all over."

"You're the first Arkansan I've met up here."

Searcy descends on us wearing his "between-acts" kimono, looking like a monstrous butterfly. "Well, well!" he says. "Knew it wouldn't take you two long to meet."

"Impressive show, Searce. The 'Conga' number from *Wonderful Town* knocked me dead. May I get you a drink?"

"Honey, you know I never touch the stuff during a performance. If I do, these lips will get a mind of their own. But," he adds, "since it's opening night and since there've been no major catastrophes thus far, I suppose a wee glass of vodka wouldn't hurt."

"And for Miss Streisand?"

"Jesus," he says.

"Pardon?"

"That's my name."

Searcy clasps his hands together, exclaiming, "So you haven't met! Well *permit moi, por favor.* Zero MacNoo, meet my latest star, Miss Jesus Las Vegas." Searcy can't help but add, "If you had been here in time to peruse your program, you'd have known that."

"I'm really sorry, Searce."

"There's nothing worse than peeking through the curtains just before they open to see your best friends aren't even at their table!"

"Don't blame me."

"Randy in another one of his moods?"

"You know how he feels about your forsaking the legit-imate stage for these dubious surroundings."

Searcy shouts at him over the crowd. "We can't all work the Stratford Festival, honey!"

Jesus and I shake hands. He has wonderful hands.

"I'll just have a beer," he says.

I motion over to Randy to see if he wants anything.

"Scotch," he growls.

"Don't you mean a mineral water?"

"I mean a scotch! And make it a double!"

After I get the bartender's attention and place our order, I resume my flirtation with Jesus. "Where'd you ever get a name like that?"

"His daddy's a tent preacher," Searcy answers for him. "And his mama's a showgirl."

"Is he making this up?"

"Not entirely." Jesus grins.

"Biggest talent I've run into in a decade!" Searcy exclaims. "This kid's got real class, Zero, unlike most of these queens. Star quality. Like me!"

"Well, it's certainly true. You don't look a thing like Streisand, and you sure had me convinced."

"Wait till you see his Sam Cooke."

"I didn't know Sam Cooke was a girl."

"One of the originals!" Searce replies, giggling gaily.

"Scotch," growls Randy from the lonesome table.

I take it over to him.

He grabs me by the arm. "As your friend, it's my duty to tell you you're on the verge of making a very big fool of yourself."

"How?" I ask innocently.

"Good thing Clay's out of town, isn't it? Go ahead. Desert me on our one night out."

I'm only half listening to Randy's tirade. The other half of me is watching Jesus put a Marlboro to his lips. "I'm not deserting you, Randy. You're just jealous I got to him first."

"I am not jealous! You just see that you keep me in the scotch. I don't even want to be here!"

Back at the bar, Jesus is asking Searcy, "How long we got till the next show?"

" 'Bout half an hour."

Jesus motions to the pool table and asks me if I want to play.

I tell him I'm terrible at pool.

"Good," he says, sauntering over. "You break." He deposits some quarters in the slot, racks up the balls, and hands me a cue.

"Dollar a game," he adds.

I position myself against the table like Paul Newman in *The Hustler*. I pocket two stripes and two solids, one of them being the eight.

Jesus laughs. "That's one dollar you owe me. This time you rack."

He pockets three solids on the break and continues dropping balls with studious concentration.

I start making small talk, hoping he'll miss a shot. "Where're ya staying?" I ask.

"Selby Hotel," he says, not looking up.

"How do you like it?"

"It's OK. But I hate not having my own kitchen."

"How long are you here for?"

"Depends on the show."

"Maybe Searcy can find you a sublet."

"He's working on it."

Before I even get a turn, Jesus is down to the eight ball.

"Top right," he calls.

He makes it.

"That's two dollars you owe me."

I reach in my pocket to pay up. He touches my hand. "Why don't you just meet me after the show and we'll settle things then?"

"Sure. I mean, we'll be here."

He smiles and disappears backstage. I go back to my seat.

"So?" asks Randy.

"So what?"

"I've seen you like this before," he says knowingly.

But I'm saved from further interrogation by the lights dimming.

The curtain opens on Searcy as Lauren Bacall in *Woman of the Year*. His three-note range matches hers perfectly. Then he does an onstage reversal of his wig and dress to become Angela Lansbury in *Sweeney Todd*. That's followed by a full-chorus rendition of "There Is Nothing Like a Dame." And finally Jesus, who performs a stunning version of "I'm Just a Little Girl from Little Rock," starting out as Carol Channing and ending up as Marilyn Monroe.

After the show, Searcy decides to take Randy off my hands. They're going down to Fran's, a twenty-four-hour dive that attracts a vast range of clientele thanks to its liquor license, all-day breakfast menu, and spaghetti cellar.

"To people-watch," says Searce. "I'm in the process of getting used to the place. We'll all end up working there once our looks go."

"Once?" leers the drunken Randy.

"Well, I don't know about yours, hon, but mine are just down in Jamaica getting a suntan, do ya mind?"

Randy weaves down the staircase and out onto Yonge Street singing, "I Enjoy Being a Girl."

"So," says Jesus Las Vegas. "Your place or mine?"

I find the assumption that we're automatically spending the night together rather bold, but I dismiss my reservations and simply say, "Mine."

Jesus pulls off his T-shirt, steps out of his jeans, and perches on the arm of the couch in just his underwear. I, of course, am still fully dressed.

We talk.

"My lover's in the air force," he tells me. "We don't see

that much of each other, but if he knew I was here tonight, he'd kill us both. What about yours?"

"No, I don't think so. He's not really the Rambo type. He's very nice. You'd like him. Everyone does."

"What's he do?"

"Investment banking."

"Sounds like a death sentence."

"Well, he gets to travel a lot, which he likes."

"So, while the cat's away—"

"Look. I didn't go out with the intention of meeting anyone tonight."

"That's what they all say." Jesus grins, displaying himself in a slightly more provocative position.

"You're awfully sure of yourself, aren't you?"

"If I don't believe in me, who will?"

That does it.

I jump him.

After a very romantic half hour on the couch, we try our luck in bed. Before I know it, he's straddled me, slipped me inside of him, no condom, and I freeze.

"What's the matter?" he asks.

"Ever heard of the health crisis?"

"Don't worry. I never do this."

"You're doing it now."

"I come from a family of faith healers." He laughs. "Nothing ever happens to me."

"Have you ever known anyone who's been sick?"

"Do you think I was born yesterday?"

"Funny." I lift him off me. "And you seemed like such a smart kid." I've lost my erection and roll away.

"God, I hate this." He pouts.

"Come on," I tell him, "it's not as bad as all that." I reach for the K-Y and grease us both up with a generous gob. "Watch me thrill you with my expert hands."

I'm awake hours before Jesus is. I busy myself cleaning the apartment, wondering what in the hell possessed me to invite a virtual stranger into Clay's bed.

I check on him every fifteen minutes to see if he's stirred. Finally at noon, I just give him a good shake and say, "Get up!"

"What's goin' on?" he asks with a start. "Your lover's not back, is he?"

"No. But it's late. Don't you eat breakfast?"

"Yeah," he says, pulling me to him. "As long as you're on the menu."

"I've got a lot of things to do today," I tell him.

"Let's just do what we did last night."

"If you insist."

"I insist."

He throws back the sheet, exposing his naked body. He's hard, ready, and raring to go.

Half an hour later, he slips on his jeans and T-shirt. He doesn't bother with his underwear. He just crams that in his back pocket like a handkerchief. Or an advertisement. I'm not sure which.

"Some kind of new code?" I ask.

"No, I just don't feel like wearing it today."

I take him down to the Church Street Café.

He orders half the menu.

"How'd you ever get into female impersonation?" I ask him.

"Like anything," he says. "I was good at it."

"But from the evangelical tents of Arkansas to Barbra Streisand?"

"I didn't start with Barbra. I started with Mary."

"Mary Martin?"

"No, you idiot, the Virgin."

"You played the Virgin Mary?"

"Yeah, it was all part of our revival routine. My mama had nine sons. Someone had to do it."

"But my semiretarded cousin and I used to spy on revivals all the time. We never once saw anybody dressed in anything other than a choir robe."

"Then you obviously didn't see us. We acted out all the biblical passages. Mama even found a way to incorporate her chorus-line kick."

"And they didn't lynch her?"

"Lynch her? Hell no. They loved it. A revival is just as much show business as anything else. You couldn't ask for better training. Plus it's a damn good living to boot. I tell you, when these looks go you can bet I won't be stuck in any two-bit restaurant. No way. That's when I get born again."

"What does your family think of your work now?"

"When I won Miss Little Rock, they sent me a case of Baby Duck. Does that tell you anything?"

"It tells me their taste in wine."

He looks at my plate. "You gonna eat your sausage?"

"No, go ahead."

He stabs it with his fork and pops it in his mouth. "Best sausage I've had in Canada so far."

"I'm glad you like it."

When the waiter brings the check, I tell Jesus it's on me.

"Thanks," he says. "And in return I'll let you off the hook for that two bucks you owe me."

"What two bucks?"

"Your pool debt."

"No," I say, handing it over. "I prefer to pay my debts."

On my grocery rounds, I run into Randy, who's sitting on the steps of the Second Cup.

"Recovering from le gym," he says.

"You joined?"

"For my health."

"You mean so you can watch all the muscle queens shower."

"One of the many fringe benefits." He takes a sip of his tea. "Did you have fun last night?"

"I suppose."

"Is that all?"

"Isn't that enough?"

"Come on, Zero. You're talking to your A-1 confidant. Either you did or you didn't."

"I just wonder if I'm not getting a little old for the mating ritual."

"Well, anytime you feel too feeble, just send 'em over to me."

"I thought you didn't trust twinkies."

"This has nothing to do with trust."

"Very funny."

"You busy tonight? Want to go to a movie?"

"Can't. I'm making a welcome-home dinner for Clay."

"My, you *do* feel guilty."

"Yes, and I'd better get home and get at it."

I curtsy.

He flexes his biceps.

God, I've missed you!" says Clay. He reaches for our toy box and hands me some rope. "Be careful, no burns, huh? I've gotta play squash with someone from work tomorrow."

I tie his hands to the headboard and bind his feet, as he requests. With my tongue, I begin to trace the entire length of his body. His cock bobbles with excitement.

The phone rings. We let the answering machine get it. After the beep, I hear my mother's voice saying, "Zero, if you're there, *please* answer. I've got some news that'll change all life as we know it."

Thinking she's won a million dollars, I dash into the living room and pick up. "Hello?"

"Hope I'm not interrupting anything."

"What's the big news?"

She takes a deep breath and announces, "I'm gettin' married!"

"You're *what?*"

"You heard me."

"To whom?"

"J.B. Who else?"

"What happened to Sparky?"

"Sparky's still Sparky. But I've waited five years, five years for that wife of his to die, and I'm not waiting any longer. There are other things in this life besides love, extravagance, and weekends on the sly."

"Like what?"

"Like I'll be sixty next year and I've gotta start thinking about some security. J.B.'s so good to me, Zero, he really is, and I *do* love him. If it wasn't for Sparky, I wouldn't know I could love any better. I've made my decision and I couldn't be happier. But best of all, J.B.'s gonna fly both you and Doll in for the big day! Now I need your address so I can send you a ticket."

"You have my address."

"Not when you move every other month."

"I don't move every other month."

"Just give it to me again and quit arguing."

I give it to her.

"Oh," she says. "Alexander Street. Well, I do have it."

"Told you so."

"I'm entitled to make a mistake every now and then, aren't I?" Her tone shifts. "Do you have anything decent to wear? I mean a suit. I don't want you showing up here dressed like a clown!"

"Don't worry, I'll get one. It's not every day your mother gets married."

"Well, get something classic. This isn't the last time I plan to go marchin' down the aisle."

"What?"

"If Sparky thinks he's gonna outlive Hilda, I'm certainly

gonna outlive J.B. He's over seventy. 'Course Aunt Tula swears he'll have a stroke the minute I say 'I do' and I'll end up having to nurse him the rest of my life."

"Then why are you marrying him? It seems to me what with Sparky, J.B., and all your other gentlemen friends you've got a pretty good thing going."

"That just shows how much you know. Now, back to your outfit. Do you have any shoes? Those orange things you wear won't go with any suit I've ever seen."

"I've still got those Weejuns you bought me the last time I was down."

"Then don't forget to bring 'em. What size are you any-way, coat-wise?"

"Forty, forty-two, depending."

"That's the same size as J.B. You know he's got a million clothes he never even touches. Once I get him moved in I'm gonna go through his closet and send you some."

"I hardly think it'd be appropriate for me to go running around in the clothes of a seventy-year-old."

"Why? They're just ordinary clothes."

"Mom, I can dress myself!"

"Well you'd never know it by looking at you!"

"When *is* this wedding anyway?"

"The last Saturday in July. Your sister's coming in on the Friday. I thought I'd get one of those pepper hams from Terry's and invite J.B.'s clan over to eat it with us."

"The sacrificial pig?"

"I'm calling it the rehearsal dinner. And just to warn you, they're a lot more reserved than we are."

"I promise not to dance naked on the table."

"I'd appreciate that. Now, why don't you come down on the Thursday so we can have us a little visit?"

"You mean so I can help you run a million errands?"

"Well, these things just don't happen by themselves, Zero. You might take a little pride in getting your old ma hitched."

"Are you asking me to be your bridesmaid?"

"Whatever. I just want you here."

"Well, I'm touched. I really am. And I'll come on the Thursday. But I'll have to see Dad at some point."

"Why? I'm paying for this, not him."

"He's still my father."

"Then see him *after* I go on my honeymoon."

"Where are y'all goin'?"

"Do you think I'd be stupid enough to tell you?"

"Why not?"

"Because I do not intend to get there and be greeted by anyone's idea of a practical joke. I mean to relax, eat my weight in shrimp, and drive the golf cart."

"What golf cart?"

"J.B.'s golf cart. He's a pro. Plays golf first thing every single day of his life."

"But you hate golf!"

"I don't any such thing and don't you forget it!" *Clunk.* She's hung up on me.

I stare listlessly at the dead receiver, wondering what I ever did to deserve a mother who can't say goodbye.

Clay calls from the bedroom, "Hurry up, will you, my foot's gone to sleep."

"As long as that's the only thing."

"Just get in here and untie me."

"Not on your life."

"Well, if you're gonna be that way about it, you might as well get me my tit clamps."

I comply.

He screams.

The torture of the Ken doll continues.

Searcy is on a campaign to move Jesus Las Vegas into Randy's.

Randy, thank god, protests. "I am too old to have a child!"

"But, hon, he'll pay rent. And shop and cook. I never heard of a better deal on a houseboy in my life. All you'd have to do is let him use your guest room. How much trouble could that possibly be?"

"Plenty!"

But three days later, Randy finally agrees. "On a trial basis," he tells me. "Besides, it'll be good having someone else around the house for a change."

For the first time in years, I do not see Randy for an entire week. He's either too tired from watching the VCR all night with Jesus, playing board games, and whatever else they get up to, to do anything in the daytime but rest.

Come Friday I call him up and say, "You're meeting me for dinner whether you like it or not."

"As long as it's something simple," he says. "Jesus is cooking his special Arkansas pot roast for when he gets home from the show tonight, and I'd better be hungry."

Randy arrives at the specified pasta bar absolutely glowing.

"You haven't looked so good in years," I say suspiciously.

"Be happy for me." He descends into his chair.

Finally it dawns on me. "You're sleeping together!"

"Is that so hard to believe?" He smiles.

"That little bastard!"

"Zero, please."

"Can't you see he's just using you?"

"So what?"

"He treats people like a convenience store. Twenty-four hours, in and out."

"He's a remarkably charming boy, and I won't have you maligning him."

"I certainly hope you're being careful."

"Of *course* we're being careful. What do you take me for?

41

Besides, he happens to be an expert on safe sex! You wouldn't believe his repertoire of tricks. Even I've learned a thing or two."

I've never eaten so fast in my life.

I tell Randy goodbye and get my ass down to Show Babies as fast as my little legs can carry me. I march right into Jesus' dressing room, slamming the door behind me.

Jesus sits at his dressing table in a Bette Midler costume, which takes me off guard. "I didn't know you did her."

"I do anybody."

"So I've noticed."

"If you're referring to Randall, I can't see that it's any of your business."

"Everything about Randall is my business."

"Well, it's nothing."

"Not to hear him tell it. I don't know what kind of games you're playing, but I know one thing, they're games."

"He's old enough to take care of himself."

"He's my best friend, and I won't have you toying with him."

"Tsk-tsk."

"And just when did you get to be such an expert on safe sex?"

"Learned everything I know from you."

"In one night?"

"And one morning."

Over the sound system come the opening bars of "The Rose."

"Shit!" hisses Jesus. "You almost made me miss my cue!"

He rushes past me, through the wings, and onto the stage. The lyrics begin, as do his lips.

Searcy pops out of his dressing room, face covered in cold cream, and wearing his kimono. "What's goin' on?" he says, confused by the sound of his music.

"I don't know," I mumble.

Searcy says to the stage manager, "That's my song he's singing out there. What's he doing?"

The stage manager shrugs helplessly. "Owner's orders."

"Turn off the tape."

"Can't, Searce."

"Yes, you can. Hit the button."

"Come on, you've still got twice the material he has. Look at the house. It's been packed ever since he came on board. The owner says we have to feature him more."

"Fine. But not with my fucking signature song!"

"Like I said, Searce, owner's orders."

For one terrible moment Searcy's face registers a grotesque expression: somewhere between betrayal, disbelief, and heartbreak. He reaches out for me and whispers, "But I've been doing that number for years."

"He's your star," says the stage manager. "And in this business, the audience dictates."

"Audience," Searcy growls, as though it were the most disgusting word in the English language.

"Even the theatre critics have come to review him. We were in the national edition of *The Globe and Mail* yesterday. Who would have ever thought?"

"And on whose groundwork? The next thing you'll be telling me is he's getting top billing."

"You didn't hear it from me."

Searcy's expression now becomes that of an enraged buffalo. He storms onstage screaming, "Who's the bitch that made this place? Who's the bitch that gets up night after night when there's only two of yous? Who's the bitch that'll still be here once that little cocksucker's gone?"

The boos roll in like waves from a distant storm. But Searcy is undaunted. And Jesus keeps right on with his performance.

Hecklers begin to yell.

"Off the stage, you fat cow."

"You're washed up!"

"The true art of the diva is knowing when to quit!"

Jesus gears up for the final bars of the song, but Searcy beats him to it, bellowing out the words in an impeccable Ethel Merman.

Very, very early the next morning, the telephone rings. Clay and I look at each other in a dazed condition.

"Do you think it's for me or do you think it's for you?"

"I think it's for you," he says.

I pad my way into the living room.

"Hello?"

"Be a sweet love," says Searce, "and meet your old gal down at Fran's for a cup of coffee."

"Searcy, have you any idea what time it is?"

"Yes, hon, and you know I wouldn't've disturbed your beauty rest if it wasn't a matter of life and death."

"Oh, god."

"Please!" he pleads.

I run my fingers through my grimy hair. "Give me fifteen minutes."

"I'll be waiting."

I find him sitting in the back corner of Fran's poking at an uneaten waffle.

"This must be bad if you can't even eat."

"I've eaten. This just happens to be my fourth. I've been sitting here all night wondering if I'm ready to fill out that waitress application."

"What happened?"

"Show Babies' owner was in the audience last night. He was so taken with my little onstage interlude with Jesus Las Vegas that he wants to add it to the act."

"Meaning?"

"We'll both be doing the same character at the same time, synching the same song, and the audience will pick their favorite by way of applause. I'm a hundred and fifty pounds overweight, Zero. How can I possibly compete with that?"

"Do Mama Cass or Roseanne Barr."

"Yeah, right. Ten years it's taken me to put a little dignity into this business. Ten years! What'll it be next, mud wrestling?"

"Why don't you just refuse?"

"I tried. I was told I could take two weeks severance pay and graze greener pastures."

"That is unbelievable."

"That's show business."

"Surely there's something we can do."

"Like what?"

"I don't know. Put Nair in Jesus' wig shampoo."

"Honey, if I were half the bitch I pretended to be I'd call Immigration on him. But it's not him I blame. Not really. It's the audience who've let it happen, the worms. They're the ones who've let me down. To think of the ladies I've introduced them to over the years, ladies they don't even deserve to know."

"But you can't quit. Like you said last night, the best revenge is to outlast 'em all."

"You're an angel for standing by me in this."

"No angel, Searce. Just your friend."

I call Randy's.

"Is Jesus there?"

"No."

"Well, where is he?"

"Gone someplace with David."

"David? What's he doing with David?"

"The beach at Hanlan's Point."

"And you didn't join them?"

"The sun's not good for me."

"Have you no parasol?"

"Yes, but if you want to know the truth, those two love-birds make me sick."

"Lovebirds?"

"You heard me. And if this aggravates my blood count, I'm throwing the little slut out."

"You sound in an excellent frame of mind."

"I am. In fact, I've just opened a bottle of champagne. Why don't you come over and join me?"

"I'm on my way."

Randy greets me at the door with a glass of Moët Chandon Brut.

"My! What happened to your budget?"

"Budgets bend to principles, my dear. One of mine being: When life seems short, only bother with the best."

"Then perhaps you can explain to me why we're all so hot and bothered by this Jesus Las Vegas?"

"Believe me, I've been giving it a lot of thought."

"And?"

"The only thing I can come up with is that he reminds us of us."

"I was afraid you were gonna say that."

"Remember when we were his age? You and me and David and Searce all slept our way through a hell of a lot of people trying to find each other. It's a peculiarity of our tribe: each gets to find his niche, like it or not."

"Well, I don't like it."

"I'd even go so far as to say that it's necessary."

"What's so necessary about it?"

"How else are we to have children?" He laughs. "At any rate, we've found our niche. We have our friends. We've made our home, for what it's worth, and we're no longer searching. Not like he is. Our future is not the open book it once was. He reminds us of what we might have missed."

"What a depressing thought. What's even more depressing is that it's probably true. But that still doesn't excuse what he's done to Searcy. I mean, to steal his signature song—"

"Zero, as an actor, I can safely tell you whenever you're given a bit, you take it, no matter who's had it beforehand."

"But it's like stealing 'Over the Rainbow' from Judy Garland."

"It is not. It's just a little drag show, on a little street, in a big city, in a big wide world."

"I see you're back in your Zen mode where nothing really matters."

"Well, it doesn't."

"I happen to admire Searcy quite genuinely. He's one of a kind. Even you have to concede that. He presents honest renditions of Broadway music, music this world is losing. And I just love how he sings on top of the tape—"

" 'The Rose' is hardly Broadway music. 'The Rose' was sung in a film."

"All right, with the exception of 'The Rose.' But you show me another drag queen who lip-synchs to Betty Comden and I'll give you a hundred bucks."

"Don't you think if you were satisfied with your own life, Jesus Las Vegas would hardly seem such an issue?"

"That's hitting below the belt."

"If you want my opinion, Zero, you need a break."

"You can say that again."

"And I don't mean a break break. I mean a break as in get-out-of-town. A breather. And alone. You've gone from eight years with David right into this thing with Clay. You've seen me to death's door and back, and I'll be the first to admit I'm not an easy friend to have. You've curtailed your own career to go to work for Maurice, of all people. And as what? A glorified secretary."

"I need the benefits. What if I should get sick?"

"I'm just saying it's no wonder someone else's success puts you on edge. The point is you don't know what to do with yourself."

"And just where'm I supposed to go to find out?"

"You're going to Arkansas, aren't you? Why don't you stay down there and house-sit your mother's apartment while she's off on her honeymoon? Lie by the pool. Get a tan. Read a few books. There's nothing like spending a little time in the place you come from to get some perspective on where you are now."

I hold my glass up for a refill and consider Randy's advice.

"You know something, I'd change my whole life if I thought I could get away with it. I'd start all over. Go back to New York. Meet the right people. Be in all the right places at all the right times. Have the eagerness I had when I was eighteen and the wisdom I have now."

"So what's stopping you?"

"Dare I say I've lost heart?"

Randy gently takes my hand. "That's an awfully honest admission."

"Well, why not, huh? Here we are with our hair down, half crocked, and it's not even noon."

"It happens. Lots of things happen."

"Once again, Randy, I think you're right about me."

"Of course I'm right. You stay down in Arkansas a few weeks, and by the time you get back, Jesus Las Vegas'll be history."

"Three weeks?" says Clay. "Just like that?"

"Well . . . you go away."

"I go away on business!"

"This is business. Sort of."

"What kind of business?"

"Thinking business."

"You can't think here?"

"You know what kind of year I've had. I've got three weeks' holidays coming. Why shouldn't I take them?"

"Did it ever dawn on you that we might take them together?"

"I haven't got the money to go someplace together."

"I've got the money."

"Well, I don't want to do it like that. You'll only end up resenting me."

"I already resent you! I happen to love you, Zero. I happen to view this as a little more than a passing in the night."

"And you think I don't?"

"I don't know what to think."

"Don't do this, Clay."

"What? What am I doing?"

"Guilting me so no matter what I decide I can't possibly enjoy it, much less benefit from it. Please try to understand. I just need some time to sort myself out."

"If you'd only tell me what there is to sort—"

"There's what to do with the rest of my life, for starters. You and my friends are the only part that makes any sense, but unfortunately that's not enough."

"Nothing's enough, to hear you tell it."

"Maybe not."

"Besides, you don't think about what to do with the rest of your life, you just do it."

"I don't."

"And I suppose this all ties in with why you can't say you love me?"

"I can say it, Clay, but there's a lot more to love than words. There's a lot more to it than habit. There's a lot more to it than just being there. And taking care. The life of two people has to go somewhere, it seems to me. It has to take off. It can't just sit comfortably in this thing you call love."

"What else is it supposed to do?"

"If I knew that, we wouldn't be having this discussion."

"Nothing's perfect, Zero. Can't you see it takes a million imperfections to make one good mistake like you and me? When are you gonna realize that? I'll tell you when. When it's too late!"

"Now you're threatening me. That's cute."

"I want a lover!"

"You want the idea of a lover. You don't want a human being with a life of his own."

"I'm trying, Zero. I really am."

"So I'm nuts, right? And if I am, far better for me to want to do something about it than just get more neurotic."

"I think the reason you can't say you love me is because you're still in love with David."

"Oh boy, that's a good one!"

"Where would you be if I really needed you?"

"I'd be right here. You know I would. I'm just going for three weeks, Clay. It's no big deal."

"No. No big deal at all," he says, picking up his gym bag.

Sunday morning, the ice between us has yet to completely thaw, though we lie in bed together drinking coffee and reading the paper.

Clay reaches for the entertainment section and opens it right to the Show Babies ad proclaiming THE BATTLE OF THE BARBRAS.

"Get this," he says. " 'Two Barbra Streisands onstage battling it out live for the ultimate authenticity in female impersonation: Miss Jesus Las Vegas vs. Miss Searcy Goldberg.' " He looks at me for a reaction.

He doesn't get one.

"Well," he says, "we can't miss that."

"I can. I hate drag."

"I thought you loved it."

"I don't know whatever gave you that idea."

He looks at me funny. Goes back to the paper and reads on. "Bet you didn't know this Jesus Las Vegas was from Little Rock, Arkansas."

"So? Thousands are."

"Don't try and tell me you're not the least bit curious."

"OK, I won't."

"But you're always complaining about how you never meet anyone from down there."

"I've changed."

"Maybe you know him."

"I do not know him!"

Clay puts the paper aside, laughing. "What's with you lately?" He turns toward me like an offering but, just as I reach for him, pulls away. "Tell me," he says.

"There's nothing to tell."

He gets up. Stretches. Goes to his closet.

He puts on his biking gear: black Spandex shorts, red tank top, and little brown gloves with no fingers.

"Where are you off to?" I ask, making my disappointment known.

"I don't know," he says distractedly. "Maybe a ride over to the island."

After he leaves, I dig around in the laundry for some of his gym clothes, bury my face in 'em, and jack off.

I walk over to David's house. He is as surprised to see me as I am to be there.

"To what do I owe this honor? Did you forget something?"

"No," I say. "I was just in the neighborhood and thought I'd drop by. Why? You busy?"

"I'm always busy."

"Well, don't let me interrupt you. Actually, I'd just like to sit in the living room awhile and do some thinking, if you don't mind."

"Fine." He looks at me oddly. "Be my guest," he says, heading back to his study.

"David?" I ask.

He stops in the doorway and turns around. "What?"

"Would you kiss me?"

He half-laughs. "I don't really feel like it."

"I know. But would you do it anyway?"

The day I leave for Little Rock the sky is full of the most ominous clouds. It's so humid you can hardly breathe.

Clay insists on taking me to lunch. He wants me to wear the suit I'm wearing to my mother's wedding, which is an old one of his we've had tailored to fit me. I meet him at the corner of Bay and Adelaide.

"Are you sure you won't let me drive you to the airport?"

"I'm sure. I hate airport goodbyes."

"Then this'll be our last date."

"Don't sound so defeatist."

"For a few weeks, I mean."

"Yes. For a few weeks."

"I just hope you accomplish whatever it is you're after."

"They why don't you wish me luck? Where are we going for lunch?"

"I've made us a reservation at Winston's."

"*The* Winston's?"

"Anything wrong with that?"

"No. Except I have a hard time enjoying food that costs as much as a month's rent."

"I didn't pick it for the food. I picked it for the table-cloths."

After checking to make sure I've got my ticket and passport, I sit down to wait for the car to come and take me out to the airport.

David drops by with a present he wants me to take to my mother. "On account of her wedding and all."

"What is it?" I ask, giving it a good shake.

"A zebra paperweight."

"Oh, my god, she'll love you forever."

"That's the idea." He smiles.

"You're a nuisance, you know that?"

"And I'll still be one when you get back." He gives me a kiss. I push him playfully out the door.

I call Randy one last time. "You be sure and take care of yourself."

"I will."

"You have the number at my mother's?"

"Right here in front of me."

"Call if anything comes up."

"Like if I die?"

"Yeah, that too."

I sit in the back seat of the Aerofleet car, restless and agitated. I can't get comfortable for the life of me.

"Quite a storm coming in," says the driver.

"Are the planes leaving on time?"

"As far as I know."

I'm almost an hour early checking in, yet still get a lousy seat.

After going through U.S. Customs I head down to the gate, take a seat in the waiting area, and look out at the runways. They're completely engulfed in clouds. Planes seem to land out of nowhere. Just *poof!* and there they are.

By the time my flight's called I've halfway decided not to fly today but to wait until tomorrow when the weather's better. Then I see the confident flight crew march down the ramp, the captain in the cockpit doing his preflight paperwork, the grandmothers and small children preboarding, and realize I'm just being paranoid.

I go over to the bank of pay phones to call Clay's office and thank him once again for the exquisite lunch, the chemistry we have beneath tablecloths, and for just being such an all-round great guy (dare I say lover?).

The receptionist informs me that he's left for the day, which is strange since he never leaves before six and it's not yet five.

"May I take a message?" she asks.

"No. No message."

He probably just had too much wine with lunch and went home to sleep it off. I dial the number there. I listen to it ring. Listen to my recorded voice on the answering machine. Debate about whether to leave a message or not and decide against it.

I board the airplane.

My middle seat is between a nun and an obese businessman. I grab a magazine and strap myself in. I pay no attention to the safety demonstration; I've seen it a million times.

The nun nervously fingers her rosary as we taxi out onto the runway.

"If it weren't safe to fly—" I start to tell her, but the businessman cuts me off.

"You think they want to refund all these tickets?" he says.

"They just send you on the next flight," I inform him.

"You think they want to go to that much trouble? Reticketing all these people?"

"Don't worry," I say to the nun. "Everything will be just fine."

The nun's brow becomes even more furrowed, and she crosses herself.

The engines roar. The plane shakes. We hurtle down the runway, full power, then lift.

There's an enormous explosion of thunder, followed by a second, then a third. I'm certain the plane has blown to bits, yet somehow we're still flying. I open my eyes. The interior is pitch dark. A crackle of lightning ignites it for an instant. Another bolt of thunder explodes. Rain pelts the windows so hard it's like being inside a car wash.

"Sweet Jesus," prays the nun, still fingering her rosary.

The call button bings nonstop. Stuck, probably. The flight attendants look at each other helplessly. If only they'd serve us a drink!

"This is First Officer Richards," says a reassuring voice over the sound system. "As you've probably noticed, we're experiencing some turbulence en route to Chicago this evening. Please remain in your—"

The plane lurches violently to the left. Then to the right. Then a quick swoop back to the left. Then straight up, engines churning with all their might.

The businessman stuffs candy bars in his mouth like there's no tomorrow. And maybe there's not.

"Father Larry warned me not to fly today," says the nun. "He warned me, but did I listen? No. I thought it was the money. He's always going by plane and sending the sisters by bus. But what I wouldn't give to be on a bus right now! What I wouldn't give!"

I reach in my backpack for my memo pad and spend the next hair-raising forty-five minutes trying to compose a will. I keep changing my mind on who to leave what, scratching it out and starting over. I finally leave Randy my collection of paintings, records, and Playbills. David my household things. Snookums my books. Searcy a couple hundred dollars for a nice, fattening dinner. Same for my mom. But what about Clay?

Clay. Why did I never tell him I loved him? Why?

Another huge burst of thunder, and the plane drops what must be forty feet. The passengers scream. Except for me. I just faint.

The fat man slaps me back to reality. "Wake up! We're all gonna die!"

The first officer, again over the sound system, chuckles. "Quite a storm out there, ladies and gentlemen, but don't you worry. We've got everything under control up here. Chicago, unfortunately, does not. They're reporting two runways flooded, so air traffic control has instructed me to circle the metropolitan area for—oh, I'd say about thirty minutes. As we're still expecting some turbulence, I must ask you to remain in your seat with your seat belt securely fastened. Flight attendants included."

The plane drops again. My stomach turns inside out. The nun emits a bloodcurdling cry, then takes a series of deep breaths. "Oh, that felt good! Did that ever feel good!"

"Do you realize how many planes must be circling Chicago in this mess?" murmurs the businessman. "Do you realize the chances of a midair collision?" He eats another candy bar.

Four rows in front of me I see the Airfone.

Could I possibly hurtle the businessman, run up the aisle, get my credit card in the slot, wait for the handset to be released, get a dial tone, dial, get Clay on the line, and blurt out "I love you" before being stopped? Doubtful. However, the next violent lurch of the aircraft convinces me to act.

The minute I go for it people start screaming. "Sit down! You'll kill us all!"

But I will not be deterred. True love knows no bounds.

I manage to get my credit card in the slot before being attacked by one of the flight attendants. She tries to restrain me, but I throw her off. I hop nervously in place, waiting for the handset to be released. When it finally is, I press the dial-tone button. With the handset pressed tightly against my ear, I listen for that precious sound.

I punch in our number. Slowly. Just like the instructions say. Some of the passengers actually start cheering. The phone rings: once, twice. Some of the passengers start yelling out numbers of their own loved ones for me to try. Then Clay picks up!

No, he doesn't. It's the goddamn answering machine again—

Christ!

I listen to my overly long and jovial message, wanting to kill myself. The first officer has somehow managed to sneak up on me. He yanks my arm behind my back. I drop the handset, screaming in pain, and stumble over some lady's legs sprawled out in the bulkhead. That's when I think I hear the beep. "I love you," I yell at the receiver, which lies all alone in the middle of the aisle. "I love you, Clay, I love you!"

"We love you, Clay!" my fellow passengers scream out in support. "We love you!"

It's a madhouse of thanksgiving as the first officer escorts me back to my seat muttering something about a straitjacket. The flight attendant hangs up the phone with a scowl, yanks my credit card out of the slot, and throws it at me.

The captain announces we've been cleared for landing. "But," he adds with trepidation, "there seems to be some problem with our landing gear. We'll be flying low past the control tower first to see if"—and this next part he says almost inaudibly—"it's in place."

"What does he mean by landing gear?" asks the nun, aghast.

"Wheels!" shouts the businessman, mopping the sweat that pours from his brow.

We whirl out of the clouds. So close to the precious ground! Then, almost immediately, swoop back up.

"Our landing gear appears to be down," announces the captain, "but whether or not it's locked in place we won't be sure of until touchdown. Flight attendants, please ensure all passengers are prepared for a crash."

Our screams are of real horror now. Finally the dreaded word has been uttered.

"Quiet, please!" the flight attendants demand with no further pretense of politeness. "Seats upright! Head between your legs! Arms crossed over your head!"

"I have to tell you," the nun whispers. "I'm not a virgin."

"Neither am I."

"I am," says the businessman, who couldn't get a thing between his legs if he tried, much less his head.

"Our final approach," announces the captain. "May I wish us all the very best of luck."

It's like sitting on knives.

No one dares breathe—

But we land!

Smooth as butter.

"A miracle!" whoops the sister. "Hallelujah!"

The businessman jiggles with merriment.

The rest of us passengers burst into applause, cheering the success of our bravery.

I swear, the first thing I'll do when I get off this bird is find a pay phone, call Clay, and leave a coherent message. The storm is still going strong. What with that and the traffic, my connection to Little Rock is bound to be delayed. I might even have time for the oyster bar. Who would've ever thought I'd live to eat oysters again?

"Thank you for flying the Friendly Skies of United," says the crew as we disembark.

I give 'em Searcy's most exaggerated "Puh-leaze!"

Once inside the terminal, I glance up at the departure monitor only to see that my connection's leaving in three minutes.

I race to the gate, run onto the plane, jump in my seat, then am informed that our departure is being delayed "a few minutes" by air traffic control. Great. The flight attendants refuse to let us back out into the airport. They refuse to let us use the Airfone. And of course they refuse to serve us a drink.

"We'll be taxiing momentarily." They smile. The liars! Two hours later we're still sitting there. Then we spend another hour sitting on the runway.

Finally, we take off. The flight is still rough, though nothing compared to the previous nightmare. Somewhere over southern Illinois, we level off.

Down the aisle comes the bar cart.

"Anything to drink?" asks the stewardess.

"Scotch. A triple."

"It's my duty to inform you that alcohol has twice the effect when you're in the Friendly Skies."

"Thank god for small favors!"

She hands me the booze with a dubious smile.

I pour all three bottles into the one plastic cup, take a sip, then mosey up to the Airfone. I put my credit card in, pull out the handset, and press for a dial tone.

I punch in our number.

Clay's bound to be home by now. It's almost midnight, and he does have to work tomorrow.

And he is.

He answers! My darling, my prince, my one.

But wait—

It's not Clay's voice that says hello. If I'm not crazy, it's Jesus Las Vegas! What have I done? Have I dialed Randy's by mistake?

"Clay?" I ask hesitantly.

"Just a minute," says Jesus.

My heart breaks as I realize what's going on, that Jesus is there with Clay. Then I hear one of my favorite Billie Holiday records playing in the background.

"Hello?" Clay says.

I try to speak: try, but no words come out.

"Hello?" he says a second time.

I try again, but it's useless. I just put the handset back in the slot, my credit card back in my pocket, and swill the rest of my drink.

Staggering back to my seat, I console myself. If I'm tough enough to survive the hazards of modern air travel, I'm tough enough to take what any man might dish out.

My sadness feels rather cozy as I fasten my seat belt around me. My own little cell, I think to myself, bought and paid for. Mine for the duration of the journey.

I look around at the other passengers, oddly comforted by the anonymity of their company.

MISSISSIPPI MUD FOLK

PART 1

Over there be a little river,
Over there 'hind them big ol' trees.
Over there be a little river flowin',
'Tween mud bottom and the breeze.

Further east be the great Mississippi,
But this be the Arkansas—
Honey, it's the saddest little river
That you ever saw.

Nobody writes books about it.
Nobody here's got nothin' to say.
'Tain't 'cause it ain't worth mentionin',
It's just nobody smart stays.

—Stellrita's Song

J.B. used to own all the movie theatres in town,"
my mother informs me, "back when we still had some,
before they all moved into the mall. That's something y'all
have in common: entertainment. Right, J.B.?"

J.B. has slid halfway down the couch, sound asleep. Mom
jabs him in the shoulder.

"I said, isn't that right, J.B.?" No answer. She shakes him
vigorously. "J.B., I want you to wake up! It's time for you
to get up and go home." Still no response. She looks at me,
makes a face, and says, "Well . . . he's just not the drinker
you and me are." Finally, she out and out screams, "*J.B.?
Do you want me to fix you a cup of coffee?*"

"Yes," he says, opening one eye, "thank you, and I'll just rest here until it's ready, if you don't mind."

"Well, I do mind! I've watched one husband sleep through a marriage and I don't intend to do it again. Now sit up and talk to my son."

"It's two in the morning."

"I know what time it is. But who can help it when a plane's five hours late?"

"I just ate too many of those fried mushrooms you kept ordering at the airport bar. The grease is killing me."

"I wasn't talking about mushrooms, J.B. I was talking about my son! I was telling him how much you liked entertainment."

"Not as much as I like golf."

"No, of course not, but the theatres you used to own. He's interested in theatre, remember? He's always writing plays. And you just better hope the next one's not about you."

"I don't write plays anymore," I tell her.

J.B. yawns. "Well, I've been retired so long I don't remember much about the entertainment business."

"I certainly hope it's not the Alzheimer's setting in." She hands him his coffee. "Here. Maybe this'll help joggle your memory."

"Sit down with me, Edie." He pats the spot next to him on the couch.

"I'm not sitting with any old man who can't remember what he did for forty years."

"Thirty-five," he corrects, pulling her onto his lap. Devilishly, he begins to tickle her.

"Stop!" she squeals. "If you don't I'll—"

"What? Wet?"

Seeing my mother and J.B. in this juvenile mode is just too much. Especially after the day I've had. It only serves to remind me of what Clay and Jesus Las Vegas are probably up to at this very moment and how badly I need some fresh air. I ask my mother if I can borrow her car.

"Sure. But where you wanta go at this hour?"

"Just for a drive."

"We don't mean to run you off," says J.B.

"It's not that. Really."

"Well," says Mom merrily, "suit yourself. Keys are on the gold cabinet."

I drive downtown to the house my great-grandfather built in 1876. It's a classic three-story place with a porch that rambles around the entire first floor. Big oak trees line the street, their branches gnarled, crooked, deformed by the humid summers and generations of deceit and misguided judgment. Ah, the Tennessee Williams in me. . . .

We all used to live there: my grandparents on the first floor, our family on the second, Aunt Lydia and my semi-retarded cousin, Trebreh, on the third.

Then, when I was fifteen, Granddaddy died. He left the place, as well as the contents of the common rooms, to Stellrita, our maid. Not that she didn't deserve it. She put more work into it than anybody. She'd also been Granddaddy's mistress for seventy years. But it liked to have killed my grandmother, Hortense, because everyone in town would finally know the only reason Granddaddy married her was because she was white. Hortense decided to live out the rest of her days at Presbyterian Village, so as not to be a burden to anyone. She didn't last long. Hated it so much she gave herself a stroke and soon left this earth altogether.

I park, still looking at the house, and get out of the car.

I see Stellrita sitting on the porch in her rocking chair, humming to herself in a gravelly wisp of a voice.

"Evenin'," I say, more to announce my presence than as a greeting.

"Evenin'," she grunts, as though my sudden appearance is not the least bit out of the ordinary.

"What are you doin' out so late?" I ask her.

"Nursin' my lung cancer by the light of a twenty-watt bulb, what does it look like?" A rage of bugs circles her head. She takes a long drag off her cigarette, exhaling the smoke through her nostrils in two even streams. "I was just thinking about you," she says. "How you was the first MacNoo not born in this house. No, your mama had Norm at home and she wasn't about to repeat the experience. Made Hortense so mad she went down to the hospital and bribed the nurse twenty-five dollars to hand you over. You wasn't but an hour old, and she carried you out to the car, drove you home, and gave you to me. Law', how you screamed, child. Minute I touched you, screams like to peel wallpaper. And you wouldn't stop at nothing short of Stell-rita's poor old dried-up tit. So I carried you upstairs and that's exactly what I gave you." She laughs. "Don't that beat all? Here I was thinking about you and you walk right out of my head and into my life. Where you been keepin' yourself?"

"Toronto."

"Is that a jail?"

"No, it's a city. A big one. Up in Canada."

"Come over here and lemme get a look at you."

I oblige.

"Ya married yet?"

I'd tell her about Clay, but I tried that once with David and you should've heard the rampage. All about how that kind of life only led to devil worship and the drinking of pig's blood. So I just say, "No, I ain't married yet."

"You and your Uncle Markus—"

"Just not the marrying kind."

She stabs out her cigarette and lights another. "Seen your daddy?"

"No, I just got in tonight."

"Well, brace yourself. He be a sad sight. Of all the people he's ever known, I'm the only one he still recognizes. And I ain't got time for him. Doctor says my mind's about to collapse. Says I just sit here havin' one stroke after another and don't even know it." Then as an afterthought, she adds, "Guess I better get on over to Beebe and check on my cemetery plot."

"Maybe I could drive you."

"When?"

"Sunday afternoon?"

"I'd fry us a chicken. Bet it's been a long time since you've had a decent piece of chicken."

"It sure has."

I move closer to the front door. "Mind if I go in and have a look around?"

"Yes, I do. Don't even I go in there anymore. Just live right out here on the porch."

"Then how do you do things like fry chicken?"

"I got my ways, don't you worry about that."

She pulls a bottle of whiskey out from under her skirt and takes a long pull. "Want some?"

"If you're offerin'."

"I'm offerin'." She hands it to me, grinning. "Hear about the government wanting to buy this house?"

"No."

"The State done named this neighborhood history. Call it the 'Quapaw Quarter' after them Quapaw Indians. You know, the ones we all got together and killed? State want to turn this whole house into the kind of hotel where they serve breakfast with the price of a bed."

"How much are they offerin'?"

"Hell, you think I'm sellin'? I need this porch a helluva lot more than I need me any money. And if this street's history, then I'm the main attraction. Stellrita be the last nigger left in this town. Once I go won't be no more." She fires up another cigarette, which throws her into a coughing fit.

"Shouldn't you try to curtail your smoking on account of your cancer?"

"My lungs are the least of my worries. I'm a hundred and twenty years old and past feeling anything. Gimme my bottle back."

I hand it to her. Her skin shines in the shadow of the light as she sets it on the empty chair beside her rocker, and I realize this is the first time I've seen her since her most recent husband died.

"Sure was sorry to hear about Trombone," I say.

"Then why didn't you write? I may not be able to read, but I know me plenty of people who can. I'll tell you why. You move on. You leave us behind. You think we just stay in the past. Or maybe you got better things to do than sit down and write your old Stellrita. She only raised you."

"If I'd known it meant so much to you—"

"Well, it don't. Don't mean a thing. And I don't give a damn."

She goes back to her bottle. Takes a sip and looks out at the street.

"Poor Trombone," she says reflectively. "Had him a wheelchair fixed up with a lawn-mower motor. Rode that thing all over town like it was a Cadillac car. I told him a hundred times to stay off the highway, but he wouldn't listen. Then sure enough, one day 'long come a Dillaham Fruit Company truck and run him down dead. Settlement only come to six hundred dollars.

"I missed him something awful at first. Missed seein' him every mornin' propped up on his cut-off arm waitin' for me just to open my eyes. Missed that so much I had to stop sleepin'. What we had between us might not have been love, but it was a pretty good substitute. He was a better man than all my other husbands put together, and I've had nine of 'em, don't forget. That's why I don't go in the house anymore. We was happy in there. It's taken me a hundred and twenty years to learn you don't mess with something happy. It's taken me a hundred and twenty years. . . ." She takes another pull off the bottle.

I press my face to the window to try to make out the parlor. The furniture is covered in plastic. Other than that, it looks just like it did: the same arrangement, the same pictures on the walls.

"Your granddaddy sure knew what he was doin' when

68

he left this place to me," she says. "If he'd've left it to Charles or Lydia they'd've sold it long time ago. It'd've been torn down and there'd be a Burger King standing here today."

"It'll still be a Burger King, Stellrita, only it'll be your kids that'll get to sell it instead of us."

"I ain't leavin' this place to my kids. All kids turn out rotten, and mine don't deserve something this good."

"Then who you leavin' it to?"

"That's between me and your granddaddy. But to hell with that. You done got me all excited about this Beebe thing. I ain't been off this porch in two years. I miss not being able to go places. I miss them dog races up by Memphis. Ever been up there? Dogs like bullets fired out of a gun. Runnin' like there's no tomorrow. And they don't even know why; it's just the way they's bred. If I were able to care for it, I'd get me a dog. A great big 'un. I'd call him after your granddaddy if I did. Walter Jackson MacNoo: dog."

"He'd be flattered."

"Have a piece of my chocolate." She points to a big chunk of it sitting on a piece of newspaper. It's covered in ants.

"Uh—no, thanks."

"Go on. It's good. Couple of colored girls from over at the mixed-up high school brung it by. It ain't poisoned. What's the matter? Lost your sweet tooth?"

"I just don't want any right now."

"Refusin' my hospitality's like callin' me a liar."

"It is not."

"It is too. What I say goes here, boy. And I want you off my porch!"

"Don't be ridiculous."

"You don't want me to have to get my gun, do you?"

"You haven't got any gun."

Before I know it, she's pulled one on me.

"What the hell are you doing?"

"Guardin' the place. Lot of crime out there, heapin' lot. And I aim to protect it from you and me and everybody else if necessary. Now go on. Git! And don't come back till you're ready to take me to Beebe."

Telephone," says Mom, shaking me awake.

I look at her quizzically, pull on my robe, and stagger to the extension in her bedroom. "Hello?" I say groggily.

"There's just the craziest message from you on the answering machine," says Clay sweetly. "When you do something, you really do it, don't you? I mean having a whole crowd of people yell out that you love me. Blew my fucking mind."

Slowly I remember the previous day's flight and the desperate message I left when I thought I was gonna die.

Then I remember my second call.

"And just where, pray tell, is Miss Jesus Las Vegas this morning?"

"Who?"

"Don't play games with me, Clay. He was there the second time I called last night. He answered the phone."

"Oh," Clay says, deflated. "So it was you."

"Yes. It was."

"I'm sorry, Zero. I shouldn't have let him answer. We were all pretty drunk."

"All?"

"Don't worry, Jim and Jon were here too. I'd been over to their place for dinner. They suggested we go down to Show Babies and catch the new act. I knew you didn't want to see it, so I went. We met Jesus in the bar afterwards, got to talking, and came back here for a drink."

"What's the matter? Don't they serve drinks at Show Babies anymore?"

"It was after last call. And why didn't you tell me you knew him?"

"What makes you think I do?"

"He walked into the apartment and said, 'Oh, you're the guy who lives with Zero.' "

"Great. Did he spend the night?"

"Don't ask."

"Dammit, Clay!"

"Well, it's not like you didn't have him first."

"That's no excuse. God! Now you sound like David. Every time I'd sleep with someone, he'd have to sleep with 'em too. I hate that!"

"Zero, will you just calm down? What I called to say was I got the craziest message on the answering machine which I don't think I'll ever erase."

"Well, isn't that sweet?" After a long pause I ask, "Are you gonna see him again?"

"We may go to a movie or something."

"I'm hanging up now."

"Come on, Zero, we can't leave it like this."

"Like what? The minute I leave town you jump in bed with my archrival."

"He is not your archrival."

"He is now!"

"Then I won't go to a movie with him."

"Go to a movie with whoever you like! What do I care?"

"Just say you'll forgive me."

"Send me a hundred dollars and I'll think about it."

"I can't believe you're actually jealous."

"I am not jealous. I'm furious! Everywhere I go that kid seems to follow. He's been through all my friends, and now he's been through you."

"We didn't get *that* close."

"I don't want hear about it, Clay. I just woke up. I haven't even had a cup of coffee."

"Do you still love me?"

"I'll have to think about that too. Goodbye." I hang up. I make my way into the kitchen feeling terrible.

"Problems?" asks my mother gleefully. She relishes problems.

"Not at all," I say, much too quickly. "That was just Clay calling to make sure I made it in OK."

"Then I trust you'll be showered, dressed, and ready to go in about half an hour?"

"Where are we going?"

"Shopping."

"But I thought we were just gonna lie by the pool today and visit."

"With me getting married tomorrow? I hate to break it to you, son, but there're a million things still to be done."

Our first stop is Norma's Night Wear. Mom asks the ancient, anorexic proprietress if she remembers me. A puzzled look crosses the old woman's face, her powdered cheeks highlighted by two circles of rouge.

"Oh, yeah," she croaks. "I remember everybody."

Mom pulls a gown down from the rack.

Norma objects. "Edie, you've been wearing those frilly things since you were twelve. It's high time you picked something with a little more sophistication. Especially for a second marriage. Take this elegant silk gown, for instance, with a matching robe."

"Oh, Norma!" Mom squeals. "It's perfectly gorgeous!"

"Yes, and rather expensive."

"We needn't worry about that. Not today. This is all going on Aunt Tula's account."

"Just my luck," Norma mutters. "Getting her to pay's like squeezing whiskey from a stone."

"Sold!" Mom beams, admiring herself in the mirror. "Sold to the blushing bride."

"Blushing?" quips Norma with a half grin. Norma can only grin in halves thanks to her most recent stroke. "Everybody knows you're only marrying him for his money."

"What?" says Mom. "Why, that's a bold-faced lie! What everybody knows is that his second wife got away with most of it, and he spends the majority of what's left supporting his good-for-nothing son!"

Norma wraps the goods in tissue paper, places them in a box, and puts the box in a bag. "Then why *are* you marrying him?"

"Because he asked me to."

Mom sashays out the door and leads us on to Friday's Florist, where we're greeted by the equally anorexic Vichtor. And yes, according to his name tag, there is an H in the spelling of his name.

His hands dart about the air in a frantic fashion. "The usual, Miz MacNoo?"

My mother, for no apparent reason, bursts into tears.

"What's the matter?" I ask her.

"He means Sparky's arrangement," she sobs. "The one he always has me pick up for the table whenever he's in town. Orchids, roses, lilies, the most beautiful things Vichtor's ever had the pleasure of putting his hands around."

"I somehow doubt that."

Vichtor looks at me with a raised brow.

Mom blows her nose loudly, then says in a pitiful tone, "No, Vichtor. Just something simple today. I'm only getting married."

"Married? Why, congratulations! Who's the lucky groom?"

"J.B." She sniffles.

"Well, I hope you'll be very happy."

"So do I, though I'm not counting on it."

"And is this to be the bridal bouquet?"

"Yes. Nothing too fancy. Wildflowers, I think. Just a few simple somethings for me to hold on to." She blows her nose again. "You remember my son, don't you?"

"No, I don't believe I've ever had the pleasure." Vichtor extends a limp hand, which I attempt to shake.

"Well, here he is!" she wails, pushing me forward. "I'll be in the car," she calls over her shoulder, running from the shop. "Finish the order for me, Zero. I just can't bring myself to do it!"

Vichtor winks. "Quite a lady, your mom."

I follow him into the work area. "Yeah."

He starts poking daisies into a Styrofoam ball. "When do you need the bouquet by?"

"Noon tomorrow."

"Do you know what color the dress is?"

"Cream."

"So tasteful."

"Well, you know her: Miss Arkansas Aristocracy, Queen of the Hillbillies."

"Stop." Vichtor giggles.

"Listen," I say on another subject altogether, "could you possibly tell me where people go to socialize these days?"

"That depends on what you're looking for," he answers coyly.

"You know what I'm looking for."

"Just checking," he says. Then back to the daisies. "There's always Discovery. It's in that warehouse down by the river. Huge place. Disco in the back, drag show up front. Used to be a lot of fun, though I haven't been there in ages. I never go out anymore except to Phoebe's, which is mainly for dykes and transsexuals, but they have fifty-cent schnapps between eight and ten and I just love schnapps."

"Good. Thanks for the info. And I'll see you tomorrow."

"I'll look forward to it."

I go out to the car and find my mother doubled over the steering wheel still heaving with sorrow.

"It's not too late to call it off."

"No. I'm going through with it. It may not be the easiest thing in the world, but it certainly won't be as hard as living as somebody's"—she searches for the right word, then blurts it out—"whore!" She wails even louder.

"Well, there's no reason you can't see Sparky on the side."

"On the side?" she replies, horrified. "I'll have you know I take marriage seriously!"

"So does Spark."

That prompts another anguished cry.

"Oh," she says, dabbing her eyes, "if he just hadn't written me that letter, this all would've been so much easier."

"What letter?"

"Just the most beautiful thing, all about our eternal love. He even compared us to butterflies, and you know I love butterflies almost as much as I love zebras."

"But did he say anything substantial?"

"What do you mean?"

"Like did he offer you any alternatives? Some kind of arrangement—"

"No. He just said he should've set me free years ago, but couldn't bring himself to do it. And that he didn't know what he'd do without me."

"I'm sure what with Hilda and his newspaper empire he'll manage to keep himself plenty occupied."

The very name "Hilda" transforms Mom's sorrow into rage.

"That woman!" she spits, revving up the motor with a vengeance. We lurch out of the parking space at a dangerous speed. "Did you see her picture in *Time* last month?"

"What was she doing in *Time*?"

"Snipping some ribbon at the Denver Ballet."

"No."

"Well, remind me to show it to you when we get home. It's right up your alley. Absolutely pickled to the gills. Sparky probably had to pay a fortune to even get it printed. And she had on some million-dollar gown you know she'll never wear again, plus that awful Doris Day wig perched on the side of her head like an abandoned bird's nest."

"I didn't know she wore wigs."

"Oh, yes. Ever since her chemo. Hasn't got a hair left on her body. But don't you worry, she'll outlive us all."

"She's been awfully nice to you, all things considered."

Mom swerves into the parking lot of Terry's grocery store. "Of course she's nice. She's no idiot." She gets out of the car, slamming the door as if to add an exclamation point to her fury, and stomps her way into the store, back toward the meat counter, with me in her wake.

"You remember my son, don't you?" she says to the butcher.

The old fellow looks at me with a blank stare. "Why, yes, ma'am, I sure do."

"Well, he's come all the way from Canada just for one of your pepper hams. How's that for a dedicated customer?"

"That's wonderful, Miz MacNoo, but we're right out of pepper hams today."

"What? I'm serving a pepper ham at my rehearsal dinner tonight!"

"Should've called beforehand. Pepper hams are in big demand."

"Called? When I've been shopping here for the last twenty years?" She fixes him with a cold stare.

Finally he mutters, "Well, I do have one on reserve for somebody I can probably put off till tomorrow, seein' as how it's your—what'd you say it was?"

"Rehearsal dinner."

"Yes, well, seein' as how it's that." He disappears into the walk-in fridge.

"I don't know why that man doesn't retire," says Mom. "There's nothing worse than living too long. I hope you'll have the good sense to put me on an iceberg with a gallon of scotch when I'm that age."

The butcher returns with the ham.

Mom takes it from him, thanking him excessively, then proceeds next door to the liquor store.

She fills a shopping cart to the brim with gin, vodka, bourbon, scotch, and tequila. "That oughta just about do it, don't you think?"

"How many people are you expecting?"

" 'Bout seven."

"Then unless it's W.C. Fields or Liquor Annie, I should say so."

Mom says to the checkout clerk, "You remember my son, don't you?"

Another blank stare. "Fine-looking young man."

"Well, children grow up so fast these days you can hardly keep up with 'em."

"I stopped growing fifteen years ago," I grumble.

"And it's been just about that long since you've been home!" She waltzes out the door into the blazing sun, leaving me to carry her two bags full of liquor.

I struggle my way into the car. She's busy aiming an air conditioning vent up between her legs. "God, it's hot!" she says. "I believe I need me something wet. How 'bout you? 'Bout ready for some lunch?"

"Sure."

"Then why don't I take us up to the Little Rock Club? It's got a great view, though the food's not much."

"Don't you have to be a member?"

"Sparky's a member," she chirps.

All the service employees at the Little Rock Club happen, in the grand tradition of the South, to be black. Mom studies the waitress as she takes our cocktail order. "Did you, by any chance, go to Central High?"

"No'm."

"Well, I'm the marimba teacher for the school district, and I could just swear I taught you."

"No'm. I don't know nothing about no 'rememba.' I'm from Camden. Just been in Little Rock a few weeks now."

"You certainly didn't waste any time getting a job."

"Just luck." She grins.

Before Mom can launch into her I-am-just-so-happy-to-see-you-young-black-girls-making-something-of-yourself-these-days, I ask, "What's good to eat?"

"Shrimp salad's always a favorite with the ladies, but the gentlemen tend to prefer the ribs. Can I get y'all something to drink first?"

"Vodka tonic for me," says Mom.

"A dry martini, straight up, with an olive. And the assorted finger sandwiches to eat. I'm not that hungry. But no mayonnaise or butter."

"I'll try the ribs," says Mom enthusiastically.

Once our drinks arrive, Mom turns to me full of expectation. "Tell me about yourself, Zero. What's new in your grand scheme of things?"

"Oh, not too much. My boyfriend. And taking care of my friend Randy."

"Is he the one with—"

I nod.

She takes a long sip. "I certainly hope you're being careful," she says. "I sure wouldn't want to see that happen to you."

I sigh uncomfortably. "Well, I've practically lived like a nun since 1983, but the virus's incubation period seems to get longer and longer."

"Like how long?"

"Some say up to fifteen years."

"Which is exactly when you quit your college and ran off to San Francisco with that Charles Manson look-alike."

"Steve did not look a thing like Charles Manson."

"How would you know? You were too drugged up to know what anybody looked like."

"I was not!"

"Are you trying to deny that you tried drugs when I know for a fact you did?"

"I might've done some experimenting, but I always did so in a responsible fashion."

"Quitting college because you have a vision on LSD is hardly what anybody could call responsible."

"For a woman who takes a tranquilizer to get up in the morning, a couple of drinks with lunch, several more with dinner, and a sleeping pill to go to sleep at night—"

"Well, I didn't do any of it until I was over thirty."

"And I haven't done any of it since I turned thirty."

"Then let's not waste our time bickering about it. What's done is done."

"Amen!"

With that, Mom polishes off her drink. Then, in a completely different tone of voice, she says, "Tell me how that nice boy David's getting along."

"Fine. Actually we see quite a bit of each other."

"I don't know why you ever had to break off with him. He was so easy to get along with."

"If he was so easy to get along with, why didn't you speak to him for the first five years we were together?"

She gives me her classic Southern belle smile, a perfect combination of innocence and viciousness.

"That's not what I call an answer," I say.

"Well, I changed, didn't I?"

"Yes," I have to admit, "you did."

The waitress brings our lunch.

"My!" Mom exclaims. "That was quick! Don't tell me the Little Rock Club's using a microwave."

"No'm. Just have it all ready for the lunch crowd. Y'all need 'nother drink?"

Mom rattles her ice cubes. "I believe I'm 'bout ready. Zero?"

"Sure, why not?"

Mom picks up a rib and takes a juicy bite. "What did you mean last night when you said you weren't writing your little plays anymore?"

"Just that. I've finally put my hobbies on hold and gotten a real job."

"But your writing could do something for you someday."

"I thought you hated my writing."

"That doesn't mean it isn't any good. You're too much like your father."

"That's funny. He'd say I was too much like you."

"Then he needs more help than I ever thought possible." She picks up another rib. "Why did I ever marry that man?"

"Because he was the brightest, most promising prospect."

"Which just goes to show what can happen to that."

"Oh, Dad wasn't that bad."

"You weren't the one chased out of the house with a saber! He's sick, and it's high time you children admitted it."

"We admit it."

"And to think I still send him an L.L. Bean gift certificate every fall so he won't freeze to death in the winter."

"You do?"

"Yes, but don't canonize me. I just do it to assuage my guilt."

"What guilt?"

"The guilt, Zero, that I might have had a little something to do with pushing him over the edge. We *all* might've."

The waitress sets the fresh drinks on the table. Mom immediately picks hers up and swills it. "Is that where you were last night? Over at the rooming house his welfare's got him living in?"

"No. I was over at Stellrita's."

"Stellrita's? Whatever for?"

"Just to see her. To say hi. And to look at the house."

"How can you refer to that sorry excuse for four walls and a roof a house?"

"It's my home."

"That house is *not* your home. That place should've been torn down years ago! Why is it every time you come down here you have to stir up the dust? Why can't you just let sleeping dogs lie? Don't you think everybody's miserable enough as it is?"

"You may have divorced the MacNoos, Mom, but I didn't. You act like that whole part of our life was some sort of freak accident."

"It was!"

"Well, I don't happen to see it that way, and I'm just as much a product of this place as you are. I'll thank you to let me decide for myself which parts belong and which don't."

Exasperated, she studies me carefully.

A slow smile breaks across her face. "Well," she says, "perhaps you are a little bit like me."

Doll flies in from Oklahoma City just in time for the rehearsal dinner. She's brought three suitcases, a hanging bag, and a makeup kit—all for the one weekend—and most of the time she'll spend running around in her underwear looking for the one thing she forgot.

J.B.'s family is represented by his shy daughter, Ferratta, her even shyer Swiss husband, and their six-year-old son. They sit, glued as a unit, on the couch sipping ice tea. J.B. sits in the armchair, a bemused smile on his face, sipping scotch.

Mom presents him with a VCR. "He didn't want a wedding ring," she explains, "so with this VCR I thee wed." The machine is already hooked up to her television.

"Why, thank you, Edie. It's just a shame you don't have any movies."

"I have one!" she exclaims. It's a compilation made from our extensive library of home movies which she had transferred to VHS a couple of Christmases ago. She pops in the video cassette and presses PLAY. The opening sequence chronicles the home birth of my brother Norm.

"Egads!" Mom screams, reaching for the remote control. "You can't possibly be interested in this!"

"No," says Ferratta, in an uncharacteristic outburst of enthusiasm. "Leave it. It's fascinating."

Mom looks at her strangely, then sits back in her chair.

We all watch as Stellrita eases my brother into the world. We watch her give him a good whack. We watch his first bath.

Mom leaves the room to go clank around in the kitchen, explaining, "Childbirth nauseates me."

Doll, in a loud booming voice, bemoans the fact that Dad stopped shooting home movies about the time she was born. Then she retrieves several of her personal scrapbooks for Ferratta and husband to view.

"Can I get anybody another drink?" asks Mom, never one to let a moment pass without food or beverage.

Doll and I are the only takers. She tops off our margaritas, warning, "Don't y'all get too drunk."

"Hell," says Doll, lighting up a Virginia Slim. "I deserve to be as drunk as possible after the week I've had. You know those musical socks I ordered, the ones that played 'Stars and Stripes Forever'? I had 'em stocked in all our stores for the Fourth of July thinking they'd go like hotcakes. But we hardly sold a pair, which makes me look like a marketing retard. Plus I swear I'm going deaf. Every time I step off a plane my ears are so clogged up I can't hear a thing." She leans her head back and administers a generous squirt of nasal spray into each nostril. This ritual is followed by a series of rapid yawns and short snorting sounds.

"Doll," says Mom. "We have a powder room for such things!"

Doll looks innocently at the gathered crowd. "Sorry. I thought we were all family."

"We are." J.B. beams. "Least we will be this time tomorrow."

"Planes bother her," Mom says.

"What?" shouts Doll.

"I said, planes bother you!" Mom moves toward the buffet. "Y'all haven't hardly touched my ham, and I practically had to pull teeth to get it."

Ferratta looks uncomfortably at her husband.

"They don't eat ham," says J.B.

"But it's not just any old ham. It's one of those free-range pigs from up on Mount Petit Jean."

"It's a Jewish thing, Edie," J.B. explains, helping himself to another slice. "And they're just a little more Jewish than I am."

"Oh," says Mom, taken aback. "Why, of course. How stupid of me. I should've thought. I mean, I didn't think!"

"This guacamole sure is good," offers Ferratta.

"Can I call her Grandma yet?" asks the six-year-old.

"Why, you precious thing!" squeals Mom, picking him up. "Of course you can!"

The phone rings.

Mom answers it on the kitchen extension, still holding the boy.

"Hello?" she says. "What? . . ." Her voice rises an octave. "Oh, my! . . ." Then she hesitates. "I mean . . . Yes! But . . . Just a minute." And she calls into the living room, "Zero, it's for you."

Puzzled, I get up. As I turn the corner to go in the kitchen, she grabs ahold of my arm and mouths, "Take it in my room."

When I pick up, the caller is in mid-monologue. "I love you," he's saying. "God, how I love you."

"Sparky?" I query.

"Zero! What have you done with Edie?"

"She's hosting her rehearsal dinner. What are you doing?"

"I can't stand by and let this happen. I thought I could, but I can't. I love her too much!"

"You're not in Little Rock, are you?"

"You bet I am!"

"Where?"

"The Capital Hotel."

"I'll be right there."

"Wonderful. I was just about to have dinner."

"I've already eaten."

"You're young. You can afford to eat again."

"You sound drunk."

"I'm never drunk!" He hangs up on me.

From the edge of the bed, I say, "Mom? May I please see you in here for a minute?"

She practically jumps through the door, having been on the other side listening the whole time.

"Well?" she asks excitedly.

"Have you completely lost your mind? If you wanted to hear from him so badly, why'd you put me on the line?"

"Because it isn't proper for a lady to talk to one gentleman friend while another's sitting in the next room."

"*Proper?*"

"Where is he, Zero?"

"Never you mind where he is! You just get back in there

and entertain those people. And turn off those damn home movies!"

I escort her back to the living room. J.B. sniffs at the air like a bloodhound. "What's goin' on?" he asks.

"Sick friend," I tell him. "Come with me, Doll. I might need your help."

Drink and cigarette in hand, Doll follows me.

Once we're in the car I tell her what's going on.

"God," she sighs. "It's just like the end of *Camelot* when Lancelot comes to rescue Guenevere off the burning stake. How do you suppose Mom does it? I haven't had a date in three years."

When we were kids, the Capital Hotel was a run-down flophouse, home to transients, derelicts, and prostitutes. Recently, in an effort to revitalize the downtown, it's been given an exquisite renovation. The marble columns, mosaic tile floors, original woodwork, grand staircase, and gilded mirrors have all been restored to their former glory.

Doll and I walk into the magnificent lobby, a wide-open space with a stained-glass skylight three floors up. The mezzanine circles it like a catwalk. That's where we find Sparky, at a small table set for his sole use.

A rack of lamb lies on his plate, untouched. "Medium rare," he says, "just like your mother would've ordered."

"Well, go ahead and eat," says Doll. "Don't let us stop you."

"I don't like lamb rare. Besides, I haven't got the appetite."

"What a waste," says Doll, eyeing the plate. "Mind if I . . . ?"

Sparky pushes the plate toward her. We both watch as Doll cuts off a chop, picks it up with her fingers, savors the smell, then quickly devours it.

Sparky rises, drink in hand, and begins pacing back and forth. "I'll be flying out first thing in the morning."

"But I thought you'd come to save her from herself," says Doll, cutting off another chop.

"With a wife and three grown kids, how can I save her?"

"Divorce."

"If only it were that simple."

"People do it all the time."

"Hilda's never given me any reason. I can't just walk out. I've loved your mother since I was fourteen. Thirty-seven years ago I showed up the night before she married your father and begged her not to do it, to wait for me. She was as stubborn then as she is now."

"Y'all sure you don't want any of this lamb? It's just delicious!"

Sparky stops pacing and grips the back of an armchair, knuckles turning white. "But I bailed her out of one marriage, and I'll bail her out of another."

"What makes you so sure you'll have to?" I ask him.

"Because we're in each other's soul, like warts."

"Why, Sparky!" Doll cries. "That's just about the most beautiful thing I've ever heard!"

"Where're they having the wedding?" he asks.

"Why?"

"So I can send some flowers. And my congratulations. To the both of them."

"At the Yoakums'," says Doll.

"J.B.'s a good man. You kids remember that. He's just not the man for your mother."

A soft tinkling bell sounds from below. Sparky opens the French doors that lead onto the terrace. "Sounds like the opening bars of 'Laura,' doesn't it? Your mother and I danced to that at our prom."

I follow him out and look over the rail to see what the sound really is. "Not the opening bars of 'Laura,' Spark. It's just that crazy man who sharpens knives."

Mom has managed to rid herself of the guests and is sitting on pins and needles awaiting our return. "Where is he?" she demands to know.

"The Capital," Doll says matter-of-factly.

"The state capitol? What's he doing there?"

"No. The Capital Hotel."

Mom gasps. "Oh, my god! I should've known. The sentimental old fool! That's where we had our prom!" She grabs her purse and car keys and heads out the door.

"You're getting married tomorrow," I remind her.

"So this is my last chance. And don't think I intend to waste it!"

I sink into the armchair, my dead grandmother's armchair, wondering why I even bothered to come home for all this. Why do I even bother, period?

What I need is to get to the nearest gay bar and stand among my own for a while.

Doll, in her rent-a-car, drops me off at Discovery. I invite her to come along but she wants to go check out the latest swingles spot. "Just to see if I still know anyone. Think you can get a ride home?"

"At the very least."

I sit at the bar drinking a beer.

An eager-beaver collegiate type comes up and says to me in a heavy twang, "You're not from 'round here, are you?"

"What makes you say that?"

"Your shoes."

I look down at my saddle-oxford sneakers, then tell him, "I used to be, but I escaped."

"Another one who went over the rainbow, huh?"

"I'd hardly call Toronto over the rainbow."

"Where's that?"

"Canada."

"Oh. I've heard it's real pretty up in Canada."

"Parts are, parts aren't."

"Just like Arkansas."

"Are you from the Chamber of Commerce or what?"

"No. I just happen to be interested in people. Sociology's my major." He shifts his weight from side to side. Undaunted by my ill humor, he asks me to dance.

"Sure," I say, surprising myself. I hate disco music, though tonight I'd try anything.

He dances like the young Elvis Presley, a lot of hip action and eye contact.

After several rousing numbers, all of which sound exactly alike, I suggest we take a break.

"Good idea."

He leads me up to the balcony. We stand in front of a giant air-conditioning vent to cool off. Our bodies fall together like two parts of the same thing. We start to kiss. And keep kissing. And caressing. Until half an hour later when he says, "Let's get out of here. Let's go someplace more private. I got me a toolshed out back of my grandma's. Got a mattress in there and everything."

Little does he know I'm suffering from a vicious outbreak of herpes, something that always happens whenever I visit home. "Sounds great, but tonight's just not the night."

He pouts, rearranging his erection.

"But listen," I say. "Why don't you give me your number, and I'll call you sometime next week?"

He writes it out. That's how I find out his name's Lance. Then he offers me a ride home.

Bingo.

Doll is planted on the couch, chain-smoking and rewatching the home movies, mostly on fast forward. "I'm glad they didn't get much footage of me. I was such an ugly kid."

I head to the kitchen and fetch us a couple of beers. "You were not. You were as cute as a bug."

"Bug? Hell, I looked like an absolute toad."

"You just have a confidence problem, Doll."

"I've got all the confidence in the world. What do I care if you got all the looks?"

I sit down next to her and make a toast. "To all the footage Dad missed."

"Hear, hear!" she says. "Like that night I came home so drunk I knocked all our childhood pictures off the wall."

"I never heard about that."

"It must've been when you ran off to California and no one was speaking to you."

"Well, what happened?"

"I was trying to propel myself up the staircase by leaning into the wall and sent every one of those damn pictures clattering to the entrance hall floor. Mom heard the racket and came out to see what was goin' on. She had on one of her see-through nightgowns and that paper hat she used to wear to protect her 'do. I was barfing real bad by then. French fries, sweet wine. She helped me to the toilet, then, when I was done, dunked my head into a sink full of cold water. That sobered me up just enough to realize I didn't have to take her bullshit anymore. I was a big girl, god-dammit. Bigger than she was."

"What'd you do? Hit her?"

"I thought about it. But I just staggered back down the staircase, past the broken pictures, and went out to the car. This was when we were living in the condo and times were bad. Dad was between jobs and we only had one car, which we certainly couldn't afford to have me wreck. So Mom came after me.

"I was pulling out of the parking space when she leapt on the hood. She flailed her arms in front of the windshield, which made me run over the curb into the two-foot flower bed. She bounced like a wild thing. I slammed the car in reverse, backed up real fast, then hit the brakes, trying to throw her off. But she just flopped toward the bumper, scrambled back up, and grabbed ahold of the windshield wipers. I turned 'em on high. She tossed from side to side, screaming, 'Stop, Doll, damn you, you're killing me!' Lights began going on in the other units. People started to yell, 'Quiet down there!' A few even started rooting: some for me, some for her.

"I sped out of the parking lot so fast Mom's nightgown blew up to her shoulders and her paper sleeping hat flew clean off her head. It wasn't until I turned onto the highway that I realized I could get my license revoked for such reckless behavior, so I swerved into the McDonald's parking lot. Mom wouldn't budge. Jesus, I thought, was I gonna have to get out and personally pry her off the hood?"

I don't know whether to laugh or cry.

"And did you?"

"I had to help her down. She was pretty shaken up, as you might imagine. Then, of all things, she said, 'I love you, Doll, don't you know that? It's your father. He's what causes us to fight.' "

"Was that true?"

"Let me put it this way." Doll stabs out her cigarette. "My biggest fear as a little girl was that Mom and Dad would get a divorce, that I'd end up taking Mom's side, and Dad would never speak to me again. Isn't that what's happened?"

"He might speak to you if you'd ever visit him."

"Well, I won't. I don't find his madness interesting like you do, Zero. It depresses me. What if it's genetic? What if it happens to us?"

I give her a little pat. "It won't." Then I change the subject. "How was your night?"

"Horrible. All anybody ever asks me is am I married yet."

"Any word from Mom?"

"Are you kidding? We can expect her about ten tomorrow morning."

Ten is exactly when Mom waltzes in. "Wasn't that something?" she says.

"Sore?" Doll asks her.

"Did he make his plane?" I query.

"Barely," Mom says, snapping open her compact.

She looks at herself in the mirror. "I certainly hope they can fit me in at the beauty parlor," she says distractedly. "I don't know how that man does it, but he always manages to ruin my hair."

Lorna Yoakum spots us in the drive, throws open the door, and steps out onto the porch, twirling around to show off her new dress. "Like it?" she asks.

"Gorgeous!" says Mom, stopping long enough to give her a peck on the cheek.

"Goes great with a gin and tonic. Can I get you one?"

"Scotch for me," says Mom, proceeding into the house to greet Aunt Tula.

Aunt Tula, Lorna's mother, is stationed in the den. She's well over ninety, enormous, and selectively deaf. She's been sitting there all day, having driven over for breakfast and to get her dress zipped up.

Tula whacks at Mom's wedding bouquet with her cane. "Did *he* give you that?"

"No. I ordered it special. I wanted something simple. Something that just looked like I picked it off the side of the road."

"Well, that's exactly what I thought you'd done."

"Pretty, isn't it?"

"Humph! Wait till you see what your married boyfriend sent."

"What?"

"In the dining room."

"You won't believe it," coos Lorna, distributing the drinks. "A wheelbarrow full of long-stemmed roses!"

"Damn! What does he think I am, a prize-winning horse? I don't even want to see them."

"Well, what am I to do with 'em?"

"Throw 'em away!"

"Five hundred dollars worth of roses?"

"I'll takes 'em for you, Miss Edie," says Dutch, poking her head out of the kitchen. "I'll takes 'em down to the cemetery. Dead folks love flowers."

Dutch has been in the Yoakums' employment for the last half century. She fusses over Doll and me, asking how we are, if we're married yet, and how many "chillens" we got. A big smile spreads across her face. Dutch, who once had the teeth of a horse, is all gums.

"What happened?"

"Had to git 'em all pulled," she says. "Personal reasons. I ordered me some new ones out of a magazine, but they ain't come yet."

"How do you eat?" asks the ever practical Doll.

"On the liquid diet," confides Dutch with a wink.

"You just mind you stay on your feet," warns Lorna, "at least until my ducks are done."

"Yes'um." Dutch disappears into the kitchen.

"Come on, bridesmaids," Mom calls. "Come help make your old ma beautiful!"

"Why does she call that boy a bridesmaid?" barks Tula. "Didn't he say he was married?"

"No, Mother, he's not married. And don't bring that up again."

A few minutes later, I walk down the hall toward the bathroom in search of some bobby pins for Mom. Aunt Tula catches a glimpse of me, bangs her cane on the floor, and says, "Haven't you got a girl yet, Zero?"

"Not yet."

"Still living with that boy you brought down here last time?"

"No, I got me a new one."

"Well, I don't see why you don't get yourself a girl!"

When J.B. arrives, Tula takes one look at him and says, "God, Edie, he's older than I am!"

"No, he's not!" Mom hollers from the guest room. "J.B.? How you holding up?"

"I'm holding."

"Lorna, fix Groom a drink."

"Gin and tonic?" asks Lorna, leading him to the bar.

"I should've been dead ten years ago," mutters Tula.

"How's my dress?" asks Mom, fidgeting in front of the mirror. "Too wrinkled?"

Doll, trying to brush Mom's hair, says, "It's fine. Now if you'd just quit bouncing around—"

"I can't help it. I'm so nervous!"

"Why? All you've gotta do's say two words. I'm the one who has to make a thank-you speech."

"Any sign of the judge, Zero?"

"Not yet."

"What time is it?"

"Still early."

"Doll, is my hair gonna take all day?"

"Not if you'd hold still!"

"Well, I need me another drink!"

"I'll get you one." I grab her empty glass.

My brother Norm bursts into the room. He's dressed like a country and western singer, the influence of his latest wife. She stands behind him, my nephew in tow. My niece has been detained by the Yoakums' piano and is banging out her own special rendition of "Here Comes the Bride."

"Will you please tell her to stop that?" asks Mom.

"Aw, she learned it just for you," says Norm, full of fatherly pride.

"Well, it's irritating."

"What a grandmother!" says Norm, encompassing Mom in a bear hug. He picks her up and swings her around the room.

Doll swats at him with the hairbrush. "I hope you realize you've just ruined an hour's work!"

Norm sets her down and says, "Hidy, Doll. Hidy, Zero. How y'all doin'? Y'all happy?"

"Been worse," I mutter.

"Well, we're happy. Real happy."

"You've sure put on some weight," observes Mom.

"That's just Barbie's good cooking," he says, patting his stomach. "Hey, kids, come on in here and give ol' Grandma a hug."

"I am *not* ol' Grandma. I happen to have a name!"

In they pour. "Ol' Grandma! Ol' Grandma!"

"Don't touch my dress! Be careful!"

I nudge my way out and head for the bar. I mix Mom a much lighter scotch, hoping she won't end up face down in the cake.

Aunt Lorna, from the kitchen, asks me if I can see Uncle Ron out back, still watering his yard.

"Yep, he's out there."

"Would you please go tell him it's time to come in and be sociable?"

Uncle Ron has the cool eyes of a friendly killer. The kind that's good with kids. I recall summer nights when he used to play ghost with us. He'd chase us around the neighborhood in a white sheet and hood and monster gloves. If he'd catch you he'd lock you in the playhouse and threaten to set you on fire. He was the best adult we had for things like that.

He greets me. "Zero, old boy. How ya doin'? Still living up there in Canada?" He pronounces "Canada" like it's some sort of disease.

"Sure am," I tell him.

"Well, I don't like the sound of that socialized medicine y'all got up there. Smacks of communism."

"Democratic socialism, we call it."

"There ain't nothin' democratic about socialism," he says. "The U-S-of-A is the only country in the world with a real democracy, and Canada had just better watch out. I'd hate for us to have to send in the troops. You tell 'em your Uncle Ron has given fair warning."

"I'll tell 'em. In the meantime, Aunt Lorna needs you to come tend bar."

I take Mom's drink back to the guest room. Ferratta is in saying hello. Mom asks her if J.B.'s good-for-nothing son is gonna do right and show up.

"I don't know," Ferratta says painfully. "Luke had to work. And he's had his driver's license suspended on account of his last wreck. But he said he was gonna see if he couldn't get one of his mechanic buddies to drive him over afterwards."

"Mechanic buddies?" says Mom with an exuberant falseness. "Won't that be fun!" I hand her her drink and go back into the living room.

I never quite know where to light at these parties. Our family's at a strange stage. All the amusing eccentrics are too old to be fun anymore, and all the middle-aged ones are too middle-aged for their eccentricities to seem amusing yet.

Unfortunately, I'm standing in the entrance hall when Judge Curly and his wife, Blu, arrive. Blu corners me right off. She plays much too much tennis, is bone thin, and has a dangerously dark suntan. "Do you know my daughter's been incarcerated in a mental institution?" she asks.

"Yes. I heard about that. I'm sorry."

"And well you should be! Her new psychiatrist says all her problems stem from that time you and your cousin Trebreh locked her in the linen closet out at the Country Club. He says all problems begin with childhood trauma."

"Blu, pardon me, but you *are* her mother and we only locked her in the linen closet once." I try to move away.

Blu grabs ahold of my arm. "How is Trebreh?" she asks.

"Fine," I answer curtly. "He moves around a lot. I haven't actually heard from him in a year or so."

"Well, Adrian, my hairdresser, says he's a big porn star. And a homosexual one to boot!"

"He's in the business, all right, though I'd hardly call him a star."

Blu makes a tsk-tsk sound. "Doesn't that beat all? I mean we all suspected you. But not Treb. He was such a masculine boy. So self-confident, self-assured, and good-looking. Always had so many girls running after him—"

"Just goes to show you can't judge a fruit by its tree."

"And to think neither one of you has come down with AIDS."

"You're as tactful as ever, Blu. I'm sure your daughter is finding the mental institution a much more positive environment than home ever was."

"My! I see you've grown the claws of a genuine bitch!" She takes a glass of champagne from Aunt Lorna's tray. "Didn't mean to hit such a sensitive nerve."

"Don't worry. I leave all sensitivity behind when I come down here."

"Ready?" Mom asks, making her grand entrance.

"I am," says the judge. "J.B.?"

"That's what we're here for."

"Freshen up your drinks, everybody, and gather round!"

The judge positions Mom and J.B. in front of the living room window, with Doll on one side and Ferratta on the other. The rest of us just crowd around wherever we can.

"Hurry up and get it over with," says Mom. "Hurry up so we can eat!"

"All right," says the judge. "By the powers vested in me, I now pronounce you man and wife."

"Is that all?" asks Mom.

"That's it," says the judge.

"Well, J.B.. Did you hear that? We're married!"

My niece launches into an encore performance of "Here Comes the Bride." Her jealous brother pulls her hair, hoping to receive the same amount of attention. When he doesn't, he starts banging on the lower register. Tula swats at them with her cane, barking, "Stop it, you little brats!"

"Mother," Lorna warns, "be nice."

"I am nice! But whatever happened to that player piano we used to have?"

A disgruntled Dutch enters from the kitchen. "S'cuse me, Miss Lorna, but I'm afraid we've got some intruders. They come 'round to the back door. I tried to fight 'em off, but they say they belong."

Luke, in a grease-stained filling station uniform, appears behind her. A hush falls over both families.

"Hi, Dad. Hi, Edie. Well, I made it."

"Great," hisses Ferratta. "You just missed the whole thing!" She walks over to the buffet, puts half a duck on her plate, and sits down to eat.

Luke's friend, from the bar, hollers, "See, Luke, I told you they'd have champagne!"

Mom slips into the kitchen to palm Dutch a five.

"What's this fer?"

"Just a little change I wanted you to have."

"Tip me after you taste the duck," Dutch says, handing it back.

"It's not a tip. It's just a little change on account of the ruckus."

"And incredible champagne at that," boasts Luke's friend, savoring the six-dollar bottle. "J.B.'s really marrying into it, isn't he?"

"Yep." Uncle Ron grins. "He sure is."

The place cards have me sitting next to Norm.

"Well—" he opens.

"Well," I reply.

"Well," he finalizes. "You OK?"

"I'm fine, Norm. And you?"

"Oh, we're really happy."

"As you said."

"Why? Aren't you?"

"I'm suspicious of happiness, if you want to know the truth."

"Ah, you just need a little place to call your own. A piece of property. We just got us a wonderful new house. Can't pay for it, but we got it."

Norm's one of those poverty-stricken doctors.

"I'm sure you'll manage."

He looks at me intently. "Barbie thinks you and I ought to open up more. After all, you're the only brother I've got. And though I never write or call it isn't because I don't love you. I just don't communicate very well."

"That's all right, Norm. I understand."

"I've been thinking about sending you something for your birthday again. I know I've missed a few years, but I want to make it up to you. I was thinking about one of those L.L. Bean gift certificates."

I just about choke.

"Biscuit?" nudges Dutch, serving from the left. My niece and nephew are unfamiliar with proper table manners. They just grab. Dutch smacks 'em for it just like she used to smack us. She really knows how to make it sting.

"Ouch!" cries my niece. "Why does she do that?"

"Elegance," Dutch says. In a word.

MISSISSIPPI
MUD FOLK

PART 2

On the front page of the morning paper is a picture of my father, standing on Main Street, pointing out the spot where the aliens talk to him.

It's the day after my mother's wedding. I have just emerged from bed with a hangover to end all hangovers. Could I possibly have had so much fun as to warrant this condition? No way. Just too much gin, too much family, and too much cheap champagne.

I tuck the newspaper under my arm and head for the kitchen. I drink myself a big glass of orange juice, then grab a cup of coffee. The first sip makes me feel like my head's about to fly off.

I sit down at the table to steady myself. Spread out the paper and look again at the picture of my father. CHARLES MACNOO, says the caption, SPACE TRAVELER OR NUT?

The phone rings.

I'm slow to answer it.

"How were the nuptials?" asks Clay.

"I don't know. I've got such a hangover I can hardly remember."

"And I've got such a raging hard-on I can't think of anything but you."

"That's a nice switch."

"Tell me what you're wearing."
"My robe."
"Is that all?"
"Yes."
"Take it off."

I keep my promise to drive Stellrita to Beebe. It's a long way, but she doesn't mind. She's got all the time in the world.

I start to tell her about the wedding, but she's already gotten the lowdown from Dutch, plus several dozen roses, which she's pinned at random all over her dress. She lights a cigarette, not bothering to ask if I mind the smoke in the close proximity of the air-conditioned car. Then she coughs half her lungs out.

"Stellrita, that sounds terrible."

"Terrible? Some people have likened my coughin' to poetry."

About five miles this side of Beebe, she says, "Down thataway. See the dirt road? That's where you turn."

The cemetery is so overgrown with weeds you can hardly see the headstones. Stellrita hops on her spindly old legs right over to her plot. She falls on her knees and emits an anguished cry.

"Is that your parents?"

"It's their grave, but they ain't in it."

"Ah, there're probably a few bones left."

"I mean they never was in it to begin with."

"What?"

"Daddy was dragged to Montgomery and back, tied to the bumper of a car, which tore Mama up so bad she broke into a thousand pieces and blew away in the next storm." Stellrita pulls a few roses off her dress and sets them on the grave.

"Bullshit. Both your parents died in their sleep."

"That's not what I told one of them reporters that come round interviewing me when the neighborhood became history. He give me twenty-five dollars for the story."

"Well, I wouldn't give you twenty-five cents for such a lie."

"Just 'cause it didn't happen to me don't mean it's a lie."

"What we oughta do is find the caretaker of this place and give him twenty-five dollars to weed your plot."

"I wanta find the caretaker so I can *sell* my plot."

"Sell it?"

"Yeah. I'm not gonna be needing it."

"Now wait a minute, Stellrita. Just because you've lived to be a hundred and twenty doesn't mean you're gonna live forever."

"No, but I'm gonna donate myself to science. Why'd you bring me out here anyway?"

"It was *your* idea."

"Well, you should've stopped me. The ground's too soft, all this death cavin' in on itself."

"You're just plum crazy and use every excuse in the book to be even more so."

"You just wait until science dissects me; then we'll see who's crazy. Maybe I'm hidin' something in here. Maybe I've got all the answers to the world." She sits on her mother's headstone and lights a cigarette.

"If you've got all the answers to the world, I'd sure appreciate you sharin' 'em with me."

"Go get our picnic. I brung you the pulley-bone special. That's what you oughta 'preciate."

"I appreciate everything you do for me, Stellrita."

I spread a blanket out on the ground, then spray myself with a generous amount of Off. "You need any?"

"Naw, the bugs don't bother me."

I ask her if she saw Dad's picture in the paper.

"Don't look at the paper," she says, chewing on a crispy thigh, "but it wouldn't surprise me to see him there. Loonies, politicians, and debutantes always get their picture in the paper."

"Then you think he's crazy too?"

"Crazier than a hoot owl. Marches by my place every day of the week. Talking to himself. Wearing an army uniform."

"Not that again! Where's he goin' now?"

"Worthen Bank. I had one of my colored girls follow him one day. He goes down there, deposits a nickel, gets back in the lineup, and withdraws it. Thinks he's living off the interest. Says it pays for his lunch every day down at Frankie's Cafeteria. But he don't pay for a thing. He just floats from table to table gatherin' up whatever people leave on their plates. Oldest trick in the book."

"And they don't throw him out?"

"Throw him out? They love him, child! Everybody loves him 'cept his own family. He's what you call a local character. He'll be more of a legend than even I am."

"I seriously doubt that."

"He's white, ain't he? And he got a helluva lot more cheers when we rode on that float together during the Sesqui-quentennial Parade."

"Sesqui*cen*tennial."

"Anyway, I raised him so I oughta know. I happen to be an expert on you MacNoos."

"I guess so."

"Never guess, boy. Guessin' be a dangerous sport."

"What's so dangerous about it?"

"Someday you might guess right."

The caretaker tells Stellrita she can't sell the plot without showing a deed.

"What do you mean, a deed? I got me a mama, a daddy, ten brothers, and ten sisters buried on that hillside."

"Then it don't sound to me like you got much left to sell."

"I got two spots worth close to a hundred and fifty dollars each."

"And I'm just supposed to believe you're who you say you are?"

"Who else would I be?"

"Got any ID?"

"I'm a hundred and twenty years old. What would I be doin' with any ID?"

"Then there ain't nothin' I can do for you until you come up with a deed."

"Tell him who I am, Zero."

"She's Stellrita," I say.

"Does Stellrita have a last name?"

"Ten of 'em," she spits. "Which one you want?"

"Whichever one's registered with the property," he says bluntly. "I'll have to do a record check and get back to you. But it'll take a couple of months."

"A couple of months?" Stellrita walks out the door, muttering, "I curse your life, stupid man."

"Go ahead and do the record check," I tell him. "Look under Baldwin, Howard, and Jefferson."

"The world's changed," says Stellrita on the drive back.

"You must have that deed somewhere."

"Forget about that deed." She starts pulling the rest of the roses off her dress and throwing 'em out the window. "Just get me back to my porch."

The fact that my father doesn't recognize anyone except Stellrita makes it easy to spy on him. I start lunching at Frankie's Cafeteria for that very purpose. I watch him the first few days from a distance. Then I walk right up to his table and ask if I may join him.

· "Help thyself, young man," he proclaims. "This is a free country, but ain't nobody gonna do it for you."

I unload my tray, giving him a quizzical look.

I take a few bites of chicken and dumplings, then comment, "Food's good here."

" 'Cept for the Jell-O. They do something to Jell-O I can't abide."

"And they overcook the roast beef."

"I like my roast done."

"Really? I had you pegged for a rare man."

"It's my wife liked it rare. Turned her into a cannibal. I eat it tough as leather now. Who the hell are you anyway to be asking me questions?"

"The name's Zero."

"Yeah, and I'm One." He laughs, practically falling out of his chair.

"Very funny. I bet you think you're the first person to ever say that."

"Nope. Ain't nothin' 'riginal about me. But whoever named you that must've had a helluva sense of humor."

"They sure did. And is your name really One?"

"That's for me to know and you to find out. But my friends call me Cap'um."

"OK, Captain."

"Not Captain. Cap'um. There's a big difference. Means I'm retired."

"Well, Cap'um, if I'm not mistaken, didn't I see your picture on the front page of Sunday's paper?"

"Wasn't that a kick? It's one thing having them aliens talking to you, but it's another thing altogether having a photographer right there to snap their picture."

"But there weren't any aliens in that picture."

"Sure there were. You just got the kind of eyes that can't see 'em."

"I take it you're not from around here."

"Here," he says, getting up, carrying his tray to the next table, and sitting down. "And now I'm from there!"

He starts in on another dish of half-eaten food, ignoring me completely until on his way out. Then he hands me a dollar bill. Only on close inspection I see it's not a dollar but a photocopy of one, with his face placed on top of George Washington's.

█ swing by the apartment, grab my bathing suit, then drive down to the river to the "gay" beach, which is really just a sandbar tucked in behind some weeds.

Who should I run into but Lance?

"Thought you said you were gonna call."

I stand on the edge of his beach towel. "I did. But your grandmother answered, and I didn't know if it was OK to leave a message or not."

"Liar." He plants his feet on my thighs.

"So I'm a shy guy."

"You didn't seem so shy last Friday night." He studies me carefully. "But I'll forgive you this once as long as you promise not to disappoint me again."

"I'll try not to. Is that good enough?"

"We'll see." He hops up and disappears into the bushes.

I follow, praying to avoid the poison ivy.

█ance and I wake the next morning, in my mother's bed, to the sound of the phone ringing.

I fumble for the receiver. "Hello?" I croak.

"Morning," says Clay. "I thought I'd call from work on account of the WATS line. How you doing?"

I uncurl myself from Lance. "Fine. And you?"

"Well, Paul's been in town with his lover. They've come to break the news to Tom's folks."

"That he's sick?"

"And that he's gay."

"Sounds like fun."

"Yeah, a barrel of laughs."

"Have you seen Randy?"

"No. I've been meaning to go over there, but I just haven't made it yet."

"I wish you would. I talked to him yesterday, and he sounded very strange."

"How strange?"

"I don't know, just distant."

"I'll make a point of it in the next couple of days. Do you miss me?"

"What kind of question is that? Of course I miss you."

"What were you doing when I called?"

"Sleeping. Why?"

"I thought I'd engage you in a little phone sex."

"Didn't you say you were at work?"

"Which makes it all the more exciting. Think we can both come before the receptionist butts in with a call?"

"It's really not a good time for me, Clay."

"Why? Do you have some hillbilly there with you?" He laughs at the very idea.

"You be sure and tell Paul I said hello. And remember to check on Randy."

"You do have someone there, don't you?"

"I'll talk to you tonight, Clay. 'Bye."

Lance sits on the edge on the bed. "Your lover?"

"I guess you could call him that." I kiss the back of his neck. Trace a circle with my tongue.

"Why do I always have to fall for the married ones?" he asks.

"Why do they always fall for you?"

"It's not funny."

I lean back against my pillow. "I didn't say it was. But don't worry, silly boy. You'll have your turn."

"It gets lonesome waitin'."

"There'll come a day when you'll eat those words."

"Are you tryin' to say there's something more important than love?"

"I'm trying to say love is a very different thing from what it's cracked up to be."

"What do you mean?"

"That's something you'll have to find out."

"Is the guy who just called a long-term thing?"

"Not yet. But I've had my share of those."

"How many?"

"Three, to be exact."

"How long was your longest?"

"I could say something crude."

"Just answer the question."

"Eight years."

"What happened?"

"Whatever happens? The passion wears off. You get too comfortable, too cozy. You become friends. You wake up one morning. You wonder if you're ever gonna fall in love again, and the idea that you might not is unbearable."

"So you left?"

"It wasn't quite that simple."

"For the guy who just called?"

"Sort of."

"Eight years is a lot of time to throw away."

"You don't throw it away."

"Still—"

"Got any better ideas?"

"Sure. Go on a little trip. Have an affair with someone like me."

"It wouldn't be enough."

"Thanks a lot."

"I don't mean it personally."

"Then what do you mean?"

"Lance, it's too early for this."

"I just want to understand, Zero."

"Well I don't want to explain."

I pull him back to me and kiss him hard.

he next day at Frankie's my father is not his usual manic self. Rather sad, strange, and preoccupied. He's not even eating. He's just sitting there, staring at the wall. I know this mood and purposefully avoid him. He eventually sees me, though, and walks over. "I feel like I'm about to have a heart attack," he says casually. "I wonder if you'd be kind enough to walk me home?"

"If you're about to have a heart attack, then someone had better call an ambulance."

"No," he says. "I'll be fine once I'm home."

I follow him out the door.

The fresh air seems to perk him up. In fact, he scampers along rather quickly for someone about to have a heart attack, merrily marching down Louisiana Street.

He lives on the top floor of an old boardinghouse. It's hot enough in there to fry the devil. His wordly possessions amount to a bed, a dresser, and an old ironing board which he's rigged up as a table. So many of my older relatives have ended up in rooms like this. After their spouse dies. After their kids betray them by moving north. After they outlive their money and other people's patience.

Dad sits on his bed.

I remain standing, close to the window. There's no breeze to speak of, but it's still the most comfortable spot.

"This is what happens when you play by the rules," Dad says. "This is what happens when the last dog is hung."

A silence falls. Then he clears his throat, and in a voice that barely betrays emotion, sings:

> There are people I don't see anymore
>   There are places I don't go
> Somebody shut the door, it wasn't me
>   I didn't fit there anymore.

"Wrote that myself," he informs me.

"It has a lovely melody. Is there more?"

"Why should there be more? That about sums it up."

"Fair enough."

"Come on over here and sit down. I want to show you something."

I oblige.

He pulls a scrapbook out from under the bed. It's filled with pictures from the Korean War. He tells me about the submarine he commanded and points out his fellow sailors who laugh from the faded pages. There's a camp sensibility to their mirth. Most of them have their shirts off and their arms around each other.

He shuts the book, and I see that his name is engraved on the cover. I point to it and say, "Is that you?"

"It's none of your business who I am."

I get up and walk back to my window. "Do you really think I don't know?"

"I don't think I care." He produces a second scrapbook.

This one is familiar. It's the one my mother kept of all our school pictures.

Dad smiles in a weird way that makes me wonder if maybe he does talk to aliens. He then proceeds to tell me all about each one of us. It's as if we stopped existing the moment the pictures were taken.

I point to my graduation shot. "You don't have to elaborate on this one. I believe I know my own face."

He looks at the picture. Then at me.

"Hey, Dad? Anyone in there? Knock-knock?"

"Who's there? I've never seen you before in my life."

"You've at least seen me at Frankie's."

"I never go to Frankie's."

"You were there today. You asked me to walk you home less than an hour ago. You were having a heart attack."

"I have the heart of a ten-year-old!"

"That's what I've always maintained. You know exactly what you're doing. You know who you are. You know your name's Charles MacNoo. And you know I'm your son."

"I have no children!"

"Oh, yeah? Then what are you doing with a scrapbook full of our pictures?"

"I bought these at the Salvation Army. And I've got a receipt to prove it!"

I start to leave. But before I can get out the door, he's

fetched his saber, unsheathed it, and chases me from the room, down the staircase, yelling, "What right have you to accuse me? What right?"

On the ground floor, a grimy woman with a cigarette hanging from the corner of her mouth says, "Quiet, space-man, or I'll have you thrown in the street with the rest of the trash!"

"You wouldn't dare!"

"Only because your brother's in here payin' another three months' rent!" She slams her door.

"I got no family!" my father yells, stomping back up to his room. "No family! You hear? No one!"

I stand on the sidewalk, dazed. What in the hell did that woman mean by "your brother's in here payin' another three months' rent"?

Through her window, I see the profile of an elderly gentleman who bears an uncanny resemblance to my Uncle Markus. I wait for him to emerge from the house. It *is* Uncle Markus.

"Zero!" he exclaims. "What are you doing here?"

"I could ask you the same thing."

He waves his hand sharply through the air as if to dismiss my question, a gesture I hate. "Family duty."

"I thought Dad's welfare paid his rent."

"*I* am your father's welfare."

"God, if Norm knew that—"

"It's none of Norm's business. I reserve the right to be my brother's keeper. Your father's been having a hard time of it lately."

"Lately?" I say sarcastically.

"He's very disoriented. It's not his fault."

"He knows exactly what he's doing. He knows just how far he can push it. Why, the last time he was in the hospital the doctors said he was the sanest man they'd ever seen."

"So you still have an answer for everything."

"Uncle Markus, he just chased me out of that room of his with Great-Grandaddy's saber. Does that sound famil-iar?"

"Lord help us. What were you doing in his room to begin with?"

"He invited me. I've been meeting him for lunch at Frankie's."

"Your father is a manic-depressive, Zero, and you are *not* a trained medical person."

"It hardly takes a trained medical person to have lunch with him."

"If he'd only stay on his medication—"

"Then we'd have a depressed old man instead of a crazy one."

"I gave that heathen woman in there something extra to try to slip it to him with his breakfast."

"Did you try talking to him? Does anybody ever try talking to him?"

"You know as well as I do that he doesn't recognize us."

"He recognizes Stellrita. Marches by her place every day of the week."

"You mean Stellrita's still alive?"

"Yes."

"And living in the house?"

"On the porch. She's had the house locked up."

"Why? Was it condemned?"

"Only by her bad memories."

"Well, I'll have to go by and see her."

"You better watch out. She'll want to know why you're not married."

He bristles.

"How long are you in town for?" I ask.

"As long as it takes," he says wearily. "And I must say I'm quite pleased to see you."

"I'm sure."

"I mean it. I'm just very tired at the moment and need to go have my nap. Perhaps you'd join me for dinner at my hotel this evening?"

"Where're you stayin'?"

"The Capital. Do you know it?"

"Do I ever."

"Then I'll expect you about seven."

"I'll be there."

He gives my sweaty T-shirt, shorts, and sneakers the once-over.

"Don't worry, Uncle Markus. I have other things to wear."

"Youth," he mutters, turning in the direction of the hotel.

At the beach, I tell Lance all about Uncle Markus. How he lived with his "friend" Jack for twenty-five years though never actually admitted what was going on between them. "We had a big falling out over that and haven't been too friendly since."

"How long ago?"

"Remember the summer of Anita Bryant?"

"Vaguely."

"Well, you were probably only ten. I, on the other hand, was twenty-one. Anyway, she got on this campaign to appeal a law in Dade County, Florida, barring discrimination based on sexual orientation. I was in Ft. Lauderdale at the time, visiting Uncle Markus and Jack. There was a big demo. I was dying to go. I'd just come out and was very enthusiastic. I'd told my whole family. I'd told Uncle Markus and Jack. I even suggested we march in the demo together. Family solidarity! Jack just beamed at me. But Uncle Markus' reaction was worse than my mother's. I rested my hand on the full-sized reproduction of Michelangelo's David, around which his entire living room was decorated, and said, 'Do you really think this has nothing to do with you?' He said, 'Nothing whatsoever.' Finally Jack piped in with, 'I'll take Zero to the demo,' and that was that. We dropped Uncle Markus off at the botanical gardens.

"It was an amazing day. Thousands of people. Men, women, kids, grannies. Rainbow flags, music, cheers, pep talks. Ever been to a big gay demo?"

"Just two hundred people when Channel Seven ran some homophobic news show."

"Well, make it a point someday. There's nothing like being in a crowd with thousands of queers. Jack was as taken with it as I was. Afterwards, we went for a bite to eat, drank a couple of pitchers of beer, and talked and talked. He was twenty years younger than my uncle. Maybe that's what made the difference.

"That night, when we got back to the condo, Uncle Markus still wasn't speaking to us. He had his dinner sent up to his room. Jack and I didn't care. We just kept talking. It was the first time anyone who'd known me as a child treated me like an adult. And boy, was I in love."

"With Jack?"

"Had been ever since I was a kid. He came to the guest room to tell me good night. I reached up and kissed him. He didn't stop me.

"The next morning at breakfast, Uncle Markus asked Jack where he'd been all night. When Jack told him, Uncle Markus threw a fit to end all fits. You would have thought I'd been jumped in the cradle. And this was coming from a man who had a complete collection of my semiretarded cousin's work in porn."

"What?"

"That's right. My cousin started doin' porn when he left home at eighteen, and my uncle had every magazine and movie he ever appeared in."

"Who's your cousin?"

"You probably know him as Billy Rockett. To me he's just Trebreh. Then again, maybe Uncle Markus has changed. For one thing he's old. And alone."

"Did Jack finally leave him?"

"No. He died. Couple of years ago. Cancer."

"Oh. I'm sorry."

"It's OK. It happens, you know. Don't think anybody gets out of this life alive."

"Well, what does your uncle do now?"

"Same thing he's always done. Works. Runs a bunch of

dinner theatres. He used to be an actor. Even won the Tony Award once. But he quit New York eons ago after he thought up the dinner theatre idea."

"He invented 'em?"

"Started the first big chain in the South. Vivian Vance in *I'm as Crazy as You Are*. Walter Brennan in *Hop-Along Heave-Ho*. And Mamie Van Doren's *Sound of Music* made the dinner theatre history books."

"Smart man."

"That's what my semiretarded cousin always maintains. I, on the other hand, preferred Uncle Markus in his New York days. Trebreh and I used to go up and visit him every summer. That's the strangest thing. When I was a kid I was his favorite. I could do no wrong in Uncle Markus' eyes. He absolutely doted on me. Then when I hit puberty it was like I was a different person."

"You probably were. Or maybe he was attracted to you and it scared him."

"No. He was definitely attracted to my semiretarded cousin, but not to me."

"What is a semiretarded cousin exactly?"

"He had a slight learning disability, but his mother insisted he was semiretarded. Aunt Lydia specialized in guilt. She'd had the German measles when she was pregnant. And Trebreh was, admittedly, a bit slow in school, but he definitely had his talents. A counselor in high school finally gave him a bunch of tests and declared him as normal as the rest of us. Aunt Lydia ended up killing herself."

"What kind of name is Trebreh?"

"Herbert spelled backwards. He always went by the backward spelling when he was semiretarded, and it sort of stuck."

"Backward spellin'?"

"Yeah. Didn't you ever do that? Your name would be Ecnal. Mine's Orez."

Lance looks at me, a bit confused. "What started this conversation?"

I think about it a minute. "Uncle Markus," I remember. "He wants me to have dinner with him, so I'll have to renege on our Mexican food plans."

"But what about the big show at Discovery?"

"Don't worry. I'll meet you there."

"You drive me crazy, you know that?"

Uncle Markus and I sit in conversational limbo until the waiter brings a bottle of champagne. I cradle my glass in my hands, savoring the bubbles.

Attempting to stay on neutral ground, I ask him about his dinner theatres.

"The business isn't what it used to be," he laments, "but I manage. *The Sound of Music* just went into its twentieth year at Daytona. The original Gretl came back on board to play the Baroness." He raises his glass. "Times change."

"They sure do."

"It's such a pity I've built an empire neither of my favorite nephews has any interest in inheriting."

"Uncle Markus, I had no idea you'd even consider leaving your theatres to Trebreh or me."

"Who else, what with Jack gone?"

I take a sip of champagne. "I bet it hasn't been easy."

"No. But fortunately I have a lot of friends who've been very kind. Too kind, in fact. I've come to learn I'm one of those strange beasts who prefers solitude. I don't wish to forget him."

I think of Randy. "Have you heard from Trebreh lately?"

"Not in a while."

"I hope he's OK."

"He is. At least enough to cash the check I send every holiday. Just as you do."

"I only stopped writing thank-you notes because you never answered them."

"One isn't supposed to answer thank-you notes."

"You know what I mean."

"No, I'm not sure that I do."

"You let me down."

"Human beings have a talent for that."

"You wouldn't even take my calls when Jack died. How do you think that made me feel?"

"How do you think I felt? I was in no shape for a fight."

"I didn't call to fight. We used to be close. I can't believe you cut me off because of one lousy weekend."

"It wasn't lousy for you."

"It wasn't a joke either."

"You were no longer a child."

"And you didn't like the adult?"

"I didn't know what to do with him. When you ran off to California you left a lot of us who wanted to help you feeling quite betrayed."

"You knew damn well why I ran off. I was in love."

"Nevertheless—"

"Nevertheless, nothing! You turned against me, Uncle Markus. You took Mom's side and acted like I was some sort of maniac when you could've helped ease the blow. But no, you didn't have the guts. For fear of being found guilty by association."

"Well, you'll be happy to know Jack became quite the activist after your infamous visit."

"You're changing the subject."

"Not exactly. He helped found AIDS Dade County before his cancer got the better of him. I now sit in his seat on the board." Uncle Markus watches my face to see how this registers.

It registers by making me feel terrible for still trying to win a battle that's a decade old. And for realizing how much I've underestimated my uncle. And how much I love him.

The boy I once was suddenly becomes the man I am, and I take his hand. Hold it. Fiddle with his pinky ring and mutter, "I'm sorry. I'm sorry for all the time we've missed."

"Perhaps we haven't missed as much as you think."

Discovery is packed. Lance bravely holds a table for us on the fourth row, much to the chagrin of several sweater fags who are obviously plotting to seize it from him. I sit down just in time.

"At last!" he cries.

"Sorry, I thought I'd never get away."

"Did you and your uncle have a good visit?"

"Beyond my wildest dreams."

The show starts immediately. The first number features three white boys as the Supremes and five dykes as the Temptations. They're just terrible. The lip-synching is all off. The choreography is completely unrehearsed. And the costumes, held together by staples, are quickly coming undone.

Then come the solos: Whitney Houston, Glen Campbell, Liza Minnelli, and Engelbert Humperdinck, god help us.

"What do you think?" Lance asks me at intermission.

"I can't decide whether I ought to be offended or not."

"By the blackface?"

"By the lack of talent!"

"Oh, don't worry," he says. "They always put the beginners in the first part. Just you wait." He smiles knowingly.

"Something to drink?" asks the waiter.

"Sure, a beer," I say, "for medicinal purposes. What about you, Lance?"

"I don't know if I oughta. I had two before you got here. I'm afraid I might get sloppy."

"Oh, get sloppy," I tell him. "Two beers," I say to the waiter. Then, back to Lance: "I've got this friend, Searcy, who's an impersonator par excellence. He really ought to come down here and open a school. Teach these kids a thing or two. Wig styling 101. Makeup 203. How-to-Pick-a-Dress-That-Looks-Right-on-a-Man. How-to-Pick-a-Suit-That-Looks-Right-on-a-Woman."

Lance just laughs. "Always the critic."

"Hey, you hardly know me."

"I've got that much figured out."

The second act, in all fairness, is much better than the first. I'm particularly impressed by a male impersonator, Dick Scorpio, who sports lamb-chop sideburns, a mustache, leisure suit, three gold chains, and authentic chest hair. She does an old Tom Jones number called "If You Love Me, Prove It!" On the second chorus, a Tina Turner drag queen throws himself at her feet, grabs ahold of her pant leg, and screams, "Work it, girl, work it!" This prompts an entire row of lesbians to hurl themselves onto the stage. By the time Scorpio gets to the end of the number, you can't even hear it, thanks to all the adoration, or see it due to the dykes stuffing dollar bills in her pants.

"Thank you," says the MC. "Thank you, Dick Scorpio. Always a pleasure. A wonderful performance, thank you very much. There's only one way I can think of to follow that. Ladies and gentlemen, we've got a very special guest for you this evening, one of Little Rock's own who's been making a big name for himself on the international circuit. He just flew in this afternoon, fresh from Toronto, Canada. Let's have a big welcome for Miss Jesus . . . Las . . . Vegas!"

The crowd explodes into a standing ovation, including Lance, who shouts, "All right!" Then to me, "Now you're gonna see a pro!"

I am simply stunned, too dumbfounded to move. Lance excitedly takes my hand.

Jesus' performance is, of course, impeccable.

Before the last of his many encores, he walks to the edge of the stage and says, "It's so nice to be home again. And I want to thank each and every one of you for coming out tonight, for supporting the rising stars at Discovery, and for helping make my career the success it is. People in other cities just don't understand. They lack your warmth. Your commitment to talent. How humble your applause makes me feel. I carry you in my heart wherever I go."

Yeah, us and the entire population of China.

I can hardly stand listening to the people around me gush. I polish off my beer feeling angrier and angrier.

When Jesus finally leaves the stage, I push myself up from the table, blaze my way through the crowd lined up outside his dressing room, and walk in to confront him.

He's seated at his dressing table ladling on the cold cream. He sees me in the mirror and says, "Zero!"

"I oughta fucking kill you."

"What?"

"I wasn't out of town eight hours before you were in bed with my boyfriend."

"Oh, for chrissake, I didn't know he was your boyfriend when I met him."

"You sure knew when you walked into our apartment."

"Well, it wasn't my idea."

"I'd rather not believe that."

"Sit down, Zero. Don't you think we have more important things to discuss?"

"Like your next conquest?"

He looks at me intently. "Then"—he pauses—"you haven't heard."

"Heard what?"

"Searcy's been trying to call you. Randy's back in the hospital."

That knocks the wind out of me. "Oh, my god. With what?"

"They don't know exactly. Some think his body's just having a hard time dealing with the medication. Some think it's meningitis. Some think he might've taken something."

The bottom drops out of my stomach. My head starts reeling.

"He's hardly been conscious," Jesus continues. "He's slept twenty-three out of the last twenty-four hours."

"When did this happen?"

"Just yesterday—"

I need some air. Pale, I run from the dressing room.

Jesus follows me. "Zero, wait—"

I run through the bar. Past Lance, who also follows me, and out into the parking lot.

"Where are you goin'?" Jesus asks.

"I should've been there!" I shout. "This wouldn't have happened if I'd've been there!"

"But wait! There're no flights till tomorrow—"

"What's goin' on?" asks Lance.

I get into my mother's car and rev up the motor.

"I thought we had a date." Lance bangs on the window. "Tell me what's the matter!"

"Sorry." It's all I can say.

I drive out of the parking lot at breakneck speed.

I stop at a filling station and call Toronto. First Searcy, who's not at home. Then Clay, who hasn't heard a word. And finally David, who's right on top of the situation and says he'll meet me at the hospital when I get in.

I drive back and forth along the river road, trying to calm myself down. It's hopeless. I go back to my mom's. I try everything: deep breathing, TV, a book, masturbation, but nothing works.

I'm going crazy. It's like I'm just about to snap. Part of me is whirling away from the other part, and the two will never meet again.

I end up at Stellrita's. She knows how badly I need her. She motions for me to sit in Trombone's old chair right next to her rocker. Her bony hand rests on my knee. Together, we watch the night.

Just before dawn, as the sky begins to turn from starry black to the deepest of blues, Stellrita finally speaks. "Up by Memphis, on the Arkansas side of the Mississippi River, be this long kind of muddy bank. You can't see it from the road or nothin' 'cause it's all overgrown with weeds and honeysuckle and things. And nobody knows about it 'cept the sharecroppers who live up 'long that way, but they're too busy bein' poor to take much notice. Along this muddy bank live what's known as the Mississippi Mud Folk.

They're just plain people like you and me, only they done give up on what people we know call livin'. They don't wear clothes. They don't eat. They just got mud and lots of it. They're covered in it. Hair all caked with it, body all caked with it. I guess you could say they become it. 'Cause when they go in the river, like they do for their mud-wrestling games, it don't even wash off. Just goes all slick-like and shiny. And they all live on this one bank as peaceful as can be. They got 'em an ex-governor's wife. An ex-movie star. Arkansas side of the Mississippi River . . .

"That's the one thing I've never been able to figure: their name. Why do you suppose they're called the Mississippi Mud Folk instead of the Arkansas Mud Folk when they're covered in and livin' on Arkansas Mud? Guess whoever called 'em that probably did so 'cause they thought it just sounded better when they was tellin' the story. 'Course, the Mud Folk don't call 'emselves anything. They don't even speak. They just look at each other: eyeball to eyeball."

"If they're so obscure, how'd you come to know 'em?"

"Me and Trombone had us some car trouble comin' home from the races one night. Wasn't a soul on the road to help us and hot as ten hells. We went down to the river to cool off and fell asleep. Woke up the next morning surrounded.

"The sight of 'em had me real scared at first, but they was nice as could be. They helped fix our car and gave us a cucumber sandwich to boot. I 'spect that riverbank of theirs is about the safest place you could be in this world."

"That's a great story, Stellrita, but if I ever repeated it to anyone I'd probably get myself locked up."

"Good. 'Cause it ain't for repeatin'. It's for your information and yours alone."

"Why do you think I need such information?"

"In case you ever have to get away and got no place to go." She pats my knee, then removes her hand. "Tell 'em Stellrita sent you. The name's enough."

She turns away from me, gazing like a lizard at the brilliant dawn.

I sit at the airport, waiting for my flight.

I stare out the window. I look at the heat on the runways. Then I stare *at* the window: at my reflection in it, and the reflection of the snack bar behind me. That's when I see my father perched on a stool eating a foot-long hot dog.

I bury my head in my paperback, hoping he doesn't see me, and wait for my flight to be called. When it is, I quickly get in the lineup.

Just as I'm about to board, someone taps me on the shoulder.

It's Dad. He doesn't say a word, he just hands me a nickel.

I close my fingers around it, tightly making a fist. "Thank you," I say. "Thank you."

BAD WIGS

"You wouldn't believe how many people we know on this floor," says David, coming into Randy's room with coffee from the coffee machine. "Joe Lowenstein, Terry Wilkes, Brandon Davies—"

"Enough," I say wearily. I sit on the corner of the bed. "When was the last time he woke?"

"Around ten this morning."

"And he didn't say anything?"

"Nope. Just opened his eyes, looked at the wall, reached up, and moved his arm from left to right."

"What do you suppose he was reaching for?"

"The great void?"

"Maybe it's the posters on the wall."

"No, he was doing it before Searcy put those up."

"Sweet of Searce to decorate the room again."

"Yes, but more for the visitors than for Randy. Like all the food people keep bringing . . . It's down in the nurses' fridge if you should get hungry. There's even a microwave."

"All the comforts of home."

"Yep."

"What time does the doctor come around?"

"About five."

"Has she said anything?"

"Only that we'll have to wait and see."

"The marvels of modern medicine." I get up and walk to the window.

David slurps his coffee. Props his feet up on the bed.

"What exactly happened?" I ask.

"He'd been feeling puny for a few days. Headaches, insomnia: the standard reaction to AZT. He'd also been fairly agitated and had pretty much confined himself to his room. Searcy and I took turns going over to check on him. Then, day before yesterday, he just sort of blanked out."

I pace around the bed. "He told me once he was stocking up on pills. He said, 'Why deny myself the humanity I'd grant a dog?' "

"Can you blame him? We've all seen enough of this to know how debilitating it is. I wouldn't want to live in a body full of poison and wrapped in diapers, would you?"

"That's not the point. At least not yet. It could be years before he's in that shape. It's his attitude."

"Maybe he needs some counseling."

"Damn right he needs some counseling. But will he go?"

"What about a support group?"

"I asked him about that too. He said, 'If I had my leg cut off would you want me to join a group for one-legged people?' "

Randy begins to stir.

"Here he goes," says David.

Randy lifts his arm. He reaches up just as David described, moves it from left to right, then drops it back on the bed.

"Like a wind-up monkey in a silent world," I say. "God, I'm tired."

"You look it," says David.

"After I heard about this I couldn't sleep last night."

"Did you get a chance to see Clay when you dropped your stuff off?"

"No, he's at work."

"On Saturday?"

"They've got some big bid due next week."

"You must be anxious to see him."

"David, don't patronize me by being nice about Clay."

"I'm not patronizing you, Zero. I'm just trying to make conversation."

"Well, pick another subject."

"How did your mother like the zebra paperweight I sent?"

"She loved it. In fact, she mentioned several times how nice you were."

"Did everybody get along?"

"For the most part."

"And for the rest of the time?"

"My family has a talent for creating more questions than they answer."

"Sometimes questions can be answers unto themselves."

"Not in Arkansas."

I reach in my pocket, pull out my money, set it on the table, and start to sort the American from the Canadian. I pick out the nickel my father gave me, a buffalo nickel dated 1955, the year I was born. I put it in a separate pocket so as not to mix it up with my other money and spend it by mistake.

"Beautiful day out there," says David. "I'll be happy to hold down the fort until Searcy gets here if you want to take a walk."

"Sure. And I'm sorry if I seem snappy."

"At least I'm used to it."

In the hallway, a very old, disoriented woman wearing only a slip shuffles toward the nurses' station. She carries a plate of food, her hospital lunch, which she slams down on the counter and barks, "Would you eat that?"

"We eat the same thing you do," says the nurse patiently. "Now go on back to your room, Mrs. Pirelli."

"My room?"

"Yes."

"I don't know where it is," she whines.

"It's right where you left it."

"But there's someone in there."

"That's because it's a room for two."

"Go to hell!" she says, tottering off in the opposite direction.

The nurse returns to her paperwork.

I hear a television blaring from a room up ahead. It turns out to be Joe Lowenstein's. The door is halfway shut, but I can see the TV and his big bare feet sticking out from under the covers. I knock.

"Come on in," he calls over the racket.

"Hi, Joe."

"Zero!" he says, muting the sound. "What a nice surprise."

"Hope I'm not interrupting anything—"

"Just some stupid movie."

"What are you in for?"

"Pneumocystis."

"The sequel?"

"Part three."

"Wouldn't know it by lookin' at you." I pull on one of his big toes.

"That's because it's my lungs that are the problem. The rest of me's fine."

He asks about Randy. I tell him nothing's changed.

"Our own personal Karen Ann Quinlan." He laughs.

"Yes. But he'll come out of it. And when he does, I'll kill him! Listen, I was just on my way downstairs. Can I bring you anything?"

"Some gum. Cinnamon, preferably. But anything with a strong flavor will do. I'm inhaling three hundred milligrams of aerosolized pentamidine every four hours. I'll never get used to the taste."

I walk down the long corridor toward the staircase. I look at the light coming through the window at the far end and think how similar it is to what people say about near-death experience. I listen to the sound of my shoes, the steady click on the old hospital linoleum. I suddenly get the sense that it's the floor and walls traveling, not me, and that no matter how fast I try to move, my body remains in the same place.

I run to the staircase as fast as I can to prove myself wrong. I run down all three flights and out into the open air.

The hospital is a long way from downtown. Halfway to Montreal, I joke. But it's on some of the loveliest grounds I've seen in the city, surrounded by acres of wooded slopes and secret paths. I walk and walk and walk.

I go to the gift shop to buy Joe's gum. When I get back to the ward, he's asleep, so I just leave it on his bedside table with a simple note: two *x*'s signed with a Z.

I go back into Randy's room feeling prepared for anything except for what I see: Randy, still out cold, propped up in bed in a Barbra Streisand wig, and Searcy snapping Polaroids.

"Hi," says Searce. "I'll be through in a minute. I just want to get a few incriminating shots to retaliate for all the rude comments he's made about me working in drag. Hold up his arms and spread his fingers apart like Babs when she's singing a ballad."

There are now six Polaroids lined up on the dresser: Randy as Barbra, Liza, Mae West, Bette Davis, Bernadette Peters, and Twiggy.

"Leave it to you, Searce."

"Well, I had to do something to cheer myself up. Did you hear they're tearing down Show Babies?"

"No!"

"The Municipal Board approved a plan for a new office tower right on our block. I've been running my royal butt off organizing protests. I tell you, honey, the Toronto of my youth has all but disappeared. If it weren't for Union Station, the Royal York Hotel, and Massey Hall, I wouldn't recognize the place. We've got to stop this development before all our hopes and dreams vanish in one great swing of the ball." Searcy cocks his head. "On second thought, it doesn't sound like a half bad way to go, does it?"

"If there's anything I can do—"

"There's plenty! I've already signed you up to sell twenty-five raffle tickets."

"Oh, Searcy, I'm terrible at selling raffle tickets. I always end up having to buy them all myself."

"Then you'll have that much better chance of winning!"

"Winning what?"

"A Labour Day trip to Provincetown."

"Just what I need."

Searcy scrutinizes my face. "I hate to say it, hon, but you're looking a little peaked. Need to borrow some of Mama's rouge?"

"No. I just didn't sleep last night."

"Then what are you doing here?"

"Trying to be of some use."

"Well, I'm on the twilight shift and Snookums is coming to spend the night—"

"Is that really necessary?"

"It's easy enough to do, so why not? We just wheel in one of the stretchers like we did last time. Make it up with some sheets and blankets. It's very cozy. So why don't you go home and get some rest?"

"All right. But if there's *any* change in his condition, you call, I don't care what time it is."

"Honey, if there's any change in his condition, you'll hear me scream from here to Saskatoon!"

I walk into the apartment so exhausted I don't even bother to unpack, shower, or open the pile of mail that's accumulated in my absence. I just throw off my clothes, get in bed, and go to sleep.

I dream of the period of time before I moved out of David's, when we bickered a lot and had very little affection for each other. But we'd often wake, in the middle of the night, making love. We'd look at each other like strangers, realize what was going on, pull away, and go back to sleep.

I dream I'm being fucked senseless. Not by David but by a large, comfortable cock that fits me to a T. It thrusts into my body. Pushes past my boundaries. Withdraws. Then thrusts again. A tongue, exact and muscular, teases my cockhead. Skilled fingers squeeze my nipples. A strong hand grips my cock and begins masturbating me. The fucking goes on and on and on. My scrotum tightens, as does the scrotum of the cock fucking me. No longer do I feel the testicles bang against my body as a loose twosome. Now they feel more like a tennis ball. The minute I come, I open my eyes.

Clay collapses on top on me. "Welcome back," he says, covering my face with kisses.

I push him away, disoriented and horrified. "What is this, some sort of rape fantasy?"

"You started it. You practically devoured me."

I move up in the bed to get him out of my body.

"Careful," he warns, holding the condom securely as he withdraws.

I'm covered in sweat and I stink. From travel, the hospital, sex. From my own putrid humanity.

Without a word, I get up and go into the bathroom. I do my best to shower a livable smell back into my skin.

When I return to bed, Clay is waiting for me, a stupid grin on his face.

"What?" I ask him.

"Nothing," he says.

"Then stop staring at me."

"I'm not staring. I'm drinking in your beauty."

I flop on my stomach, scrunch up my pillow, and try to get comfortable. "You said you were gonna check on Randy."

"Randy had plenty of people checking on him. I had my hands full with my own sick friends."

"Your friends, my friends—do you think we'll ever have 'our' friends?"

"When did you get so pessimistic?"

"I've always been pessimistic. Or didn't you ever notice?"

Clay reaches for the light, turns it off, and rolls away from me.

I've successfully managed to kill his humor and his patience, which I immediately regret.

Gently, I touch Clay's back. It makes him wince.

"I'm sorry," I say, lips against his skin.

"It's OK," he replies, as many miles away from me as I was from him.

The next morning, Clay and I have a very civil breakfast out on the balcony. Then he hands me a folded bunch of papers.

"What's this?" I ask.

"Call it a coming-home surprise."

"I don't like surprises. It looks very official. What is it?"

"A condo."

"A what?"

"I bought one. We move September first."

"Are you crazy?"

"No, actually I've been thinking about it for some time."

"How come I never knew that?"

"It's been on hold for a while. Look at the housing market."

"I don't know a damn thing about the housing market."

"Jim and Jon have a friend in real estate law who told me about the deal. I went and looked at it and couldn't resist."

"Just like that?"

"Don't worry, Zero. You're gonna love it. It has twice the room we now have. Plus a fireplace, a backyard, a deck, and it's on one of the loveliest little streets."

"Where?"

"Out Gerrard."

"Well." I sit back in my chair. "Congratulations. Or is there something else you say when people buy condos?"

"Congratulations will do," he says. "I'm anxious for you to see it."

"Yeah, so am I. But I'll be at the hospital all afternoon. How 'bout this evening?"

"Fine."

"Pick me up at the visitors' entrance about five-thirty?"

"Sure."

I pour some milk over my cereal and resume eating.

Clay touches my hand. "I'm really glad you're home."

"Thanks," I say, wondering what the hell that word means anyway. Then, quickly I add, "Me too."

"Welcome home, precious!" says Snookums, the minute I walk into the hospital room. Snookums is surrounded by back issues of *National Geographic* open to various exotic locales.

"Where did all those come from?"

"Randy's mother drove up from St. Catharine's this morning. Brought them for the ward. Plus a ton of sweets."

"That was nice of her."

"Yes. And why did it come as such a surprise to find out she's Chinese?"

"She's not Chinese. She was born in Alberta."

"Well, excuse me, but she certainly has Chinese features. She could play Turandot without the slightest makeup. Was Randy adopted?"

"No, but he has a Brit WASP for a father. Actually, he doesn't look much like either of 'em."

"That must be what accounts for his worldly flare."

"Must be. And if those magazines are for the ward, what are they doing here?"

"I'm browsing, if you don't mind. I'm planning to take a long trip as soon as I graduate from AA. A honeymoon."

"And who's the lucky groom?"

"Don't know. Haven't been fortunate enough to meet him yet. But if you hear of anyone who's available, let me know."

"Will do."

"This is my favorite." He holds up a center spread of

Greece. "Home of Alexander the Great, Plato, Socrates, Homer, not to mention those marvelous islands!"

"Yes, I've been there. David and I went the year we met."

"Really? I never knew that."

"There're a lot of things you don't know about us, Snookums."

"Don't say that, precious. It makes me want a drink."

"How's our Sleeping Beauty?"

"Still sleeping and still beautiful. There've been some very interesting developments at the office," he continues. "You ought to drop by sometime for a little visit."

"About the only thing I decided while I was away is that I'm not going back to that office."

"I have a couple of ideas that I think might interest you."

"Like what?"

"Stop by and we'll discuss business during business hours."

"When?"

"Whenever suits you." Snookums starts collecting the magazines and hauls them out to the lounge. He catches a glimpse of himself in the mirror and stops to straighten his hairpiece.

"Did you ever consider getting one of those that fits?"

"Too tight, precious. Much too tight."

I spend my afternoon alone with Randy thinking things I'd rather not be thinking at all. I snoop through the cards people have brought. I wet a washrag and dab his face. Stroke his hair. Hold his lifeless hand.

The doctor and her gang of interns barrel in about four o'clock. They poke and prod at him, read his vital signs chart, and confer among themselves. On their way out, they acknowledge my presence. "Oh," says the doctor in her usual brittle tone. "Hello."

"How's he doing?" I ask.

"Stable."

"Did anyone mention the possibility that he might've taken something?"

"Yes."

"Well, what do you think?"

"It's hard to know."

"But to just sleep like this—"

"Sleep can't hurt him."

"But what if he has some exotic infection you haven't tested for?"

"Most infections related to this disease are quite common. There's no sign of pneumocystis. No sign of toxoplasmosis. So I'm still treating him for meningitis."

"Does that mean he has it?"

"That's what it looks like to me."

"What about herpes on the brain? I've read where that can cause this sort of stupor."

"You don't trust me, do you, Zero?"

"I'm just asking all the questions I know to ask. If it were your friend, wouldn't you?"

"You have to trust me."

"Stop saying that!"

"Kicking the wall, are we?"

"Look. I just want to know what we do."

"We wait. We watch. We observe. And, hopefully, we learn. Don't worry. Medicine is full of the unexplainable."

I fold my arms across my chest, unsatisfied with her answer. "I think he did take something. Sleeping pills, tranquilizers, maybe both. And they reacted with everything else he's on—"

"Well," she says, "your guess is as good as mine." Then she leads her troops on to the next patient.

I wander down to Lowenstein's room. Again, he's got the TV going full blast.

"Hi, handsome. How you feelin'?"

"Ah, fair to middling. How's Randall?"

"Still sleeping. May I talk to you a few minutes?"

"Sure."

I shut the door and speak quietly. "Do you have the same doctor he does?"

"She's got the whole ward. Why?"

"How do you get along with her?"

"She's OK. Has a problem with queers, but at least she's up front about it. I also see one of the gay HIV specialists downtown when I'm not in hospital. They're much more positive. Tend to have a little more vested interest, if you know what I mean. They read more. Know what's being done around the globe."

"I wish Randy would go see one of them."

"Why won't he?"

"He has a general hatred of doctors. Plus he doesn't want to think about it. Doesn't want to make this the focal point of the rest of his life."

"Well, that's up to him. But it seems pretty silly not to take advantage of what's out there."

I turn my attention to the TV. It's an old black-and-white movie. "What are you watchin'?"

"*San Francisco*. Jeanette MacDonald, Spencer Tracy, and one hell of an earthquake. Care to join me?"

"Sure. I could use a little San Francisco."

Joe scoots over, making a space for me on the bed. He throws an arm around my shoulder.

A million years ago, for about two weeks, Joe and I were quite the item. I snuggle into his armpit, remembering that time, then lean my head against his pneumonia-filled chest.

Clay picks me up at the appointed hour. We drive from the hospital, down the Don Valley Parkway to Gerrard, and turn east. We drive forever, it seems, until we reach that "lovely street" where Clay has decided we should move.

Tucked in behind some shady trees and an iron fence lies a big two-story house, in the midst of condo renovation.

"What do you think?" asks Clay.

"Kind of far from town, isn't it, honey?"

"Who needs town when we've got this?"

"But I didn't even see a corner store."

"There's a corner store three blocks down. This is what you call a neighborhood, Zero."

"A neighborhood is something with a greengrocer, a butcher, a movie theatre, and a subway out."

"Come on, city boy. Let me show you around."

We look at the living room, the kitchen, the deck, the yard, then go up the stairs, beneath the skylights, to the study, the guest room, and finally the bedroom. He shows me where the bed will go. Where my dresser will be and where he's gonna put his. He's even got the dry-mounted train posters hung.

He comes toward me. Sweetly. A twinkle in his eye and we kiss.

He fumbles with my jeans.

"Not here," I say.

He drops to his knees to get a rise out of me, then pulls me to him. Before I know it, we're sixty-nine-ing on the sawdusty floor. Pantless, sockless, shoeless. His cock fills my throat. His strong legs wrap around my shoulders.

He's close. I play with his butt. His asshole practically swallows my thumb. I trigger his prostate and he flies. Sweet cum drizzling on my taste buds. My one concession to the old days of sex.

Usually we come at the same time. But today, I want to outlast him.

I stroke his legs. Play with his toes. The feeling gets better and better the harder he works. His cock begins to soften in my mouth. I let go of it to suck his balls. His phallus flops against my cheek, gummy and red. I smell him. I'm ready. I could strangle him with my enthusiasm and thrust so far down his throat he gags. He loves it. And he knows just how to finish me off. How to hold me there.

"Well," I comment, as we dress, "at least we know the suburbs don't make us impotent."

"This is *not* the suburbs, Zero. It's technically part of the Beaches."

"This is nowhere near the lake."

"I said technically."

"It's very pretty, Clay. But not half as pretty as you."

A pleasant silence accompanies us on the drive back until he ruins it by turning on the radio.

I look at the traffic. I begin to trace his inseam, up and down his thigh. "I can't believe you actually bought that place without even talking to me about it first."

"I didn't want you to feel you had to chip in. I know you don't make as much money as I do and I want this to be *my* purchase. If you want to know the truth, you were the deciding factor that made me go ahead and buy it."

"Me?"

"All that stuff you've been saying about time to yourself and a space of your own. Well, here it is! And it's a damn good investment."

"You sound like my brother, Norm."

"We've got to live somewhere, Zero."

"Yes," I admit, "we certainly do."

I say no more. Just smile.

Clay assumes the smile means we're in agreement.

I don't correct him. Why should I? I like knowing things he doesn't.

Randy is wide awake, sitting up in bed and clicking the remote control at the television set. "To think they'd preempt *That Girl* with a goddamn Blue Jays game."

"Randy! You're awake!"

"What'd you fucking expect? That I'd sleep out the century?"

"Well, it's been a couple of weeks. How are you?"

"Rested, thank you very much. And you?"

"Relieved. There are those among us who thought you wouldn't make it."

"Then the joke's on them." He clicks off the TV, swings his legs out of bed. "Help me walk. My muscles are like putty. I've been on the phone to my agent twice today. My film starts in three weeks. But luckily the shooting schedule's been altered. We're doing the interiors here in town before moving out to Vancouver for the location work. I've gotta get my legs back and I've gotta gain twenty pounds. Has my mother been bringing the sweets?"

"Yes. But you look fabulous."

"You need your head examined."

We walk out into the hallway. Down the corridor. Past Joe's room, which I notice is empty.

"Thank god he finally got out."

"Yeah, feet first."

"Oh, shit—"

"I woke up just in time to hear some crazy lady scream, 'They've killed another one!' She was wandering around in a slip. I feel like I've been living inside an impenetrable shell."

"You have. Would you mind trying to explain to me what happened?"

"I wish I knew. I was having terrible headaches, and no matter how much codeine I took, they still wouldn't let up. I couldn't sleep. I was taking pills for that too. I just kept taking more and more and more—"

"Why didn't you tell me about this when I called?"

"I didn't want to ruin your holiday."

"Hell of a time you picked to become a considerate guy."

"You worry about me too much, Zero."

"Do you even remember being brought to the hospital?"

"Vaguely. Most of all I remember seeing people around me like light. Golden ghosts. I kept trying to slip away, but

I was attached to them like strings to a marionette. I kept seeing this three-dimensional picture book in front of me. I'd reach up, turn a page, and the whole world would change."

We walk by the elevator. Searcy steps off in full drag.

"Oh, my god," says Randy. "Tell me it's a nightmare!"

"Never in my life did I think I'd live to see the day I'd actually relish hearing one of your insults!" Searcy pulls Randy to him in a hug.

"What a horrible-smelling perfume." Randy gags, backing away.

"Eau de skunk," says Searce. "I wore it to meet with the mayor. We had three hundred and fifty drag queens march from Show Babies to City Hall. We stormed his office. Made certain he realized that tearing down our little theatre was gonna force us out onto the streets. Somehow, I don't think we quite fit into his image of Toronto-the-Good. He turned absolutely green. Looked like he was about to faint on the spot."

"With three hundred and fifty drag queens in eau de skunk," says Randy, "it's no wonder."

"What were your demands?" I ask.

"Simply that the city find us another home, centrally located and with equivalent rent, else we'll take to the public stage in Nathan Phillips Square. *And* we plan to show up at City Hall every afternoon until a suitable settlement has been reached."

"Get me back to my room," mutters Randy.

The doctor is keeping Randy in the hospital another five or six days for tests and observation.

She asks me into her office for a consultation. "I think it would be a good idea if you could arange to stay with him for the first week or so after he's out."

"Why?"

"Just to make sure he eats right. Stays on his medication. Doesn't overdo it."

"He won't like that."

"He won't like being back in the hospital again either."

"Do you know about this movie he's got coming up?"

"Yes."

"Do you think he'll be in good enough shape?"

"Absolutely," she says. "I just want to make sure nothing comes along in the meantime to get in his way."

For the first time since Randy went in the hospital, I feel something for Dr. Susan Fieldstone besides disdain.

Randy, of course, wants to go home immediately and has a fit. "I'm well," he says. "I'm awake, aren't I? Do they think I'm gonna be any more well here than at home?"

"I'm not the doctor, Randy. It wasn't my decision."

"What did she say?"

I tell him.

"Well. Isn't that nice? What the fuck's a few more days anyway? It'll give me a good chance to study the screenplay. Work on my lines. My character. Gain my weight back. How 'bout bringing me another tin of my mom's cookies?"

Searcy and I take turns calling everybody to tell them the good news. Then I go home to tell Clay personally.

He's so immersed in the cursed Blue Jays game that he actually shushes me. He's lying on the couch in his underwear, drinking a beer. I jump him. It fizzes over onto his chest. I straddle him and start to lick it off.

"Zero—" he says.

"I hate baseball!" I growl.

"Then don't watch it."

I disappear into the guest room with a book.

Again, that night, I wake to Clay fucking me. Only this time it's not weird. It's wonderful. Sensation far beyond my control to the point where I forget myself entirely. I just lie there for him. And, when he's done, return the favor.

Snuggling in bed, we talk.

I tell him about staying over at Randy's and say, "You could stay with me if you want."

"I don't think so," he says.

"Why not?"

"Randy doesn't like me."

"He does too."

"Then why's he always so condescending? Either that or he completely ignores me, which is worse."

"He's just being protective. He only acts that way because he's afraid."

"Randy? Afraid? Of what?"

"I don't know. The same thing that gets us all. The endless yearning of the soul, I guess."

"My soul doesn't yearn."

"That's what I like about you."

"You know, you could be a much simpler person if you wanted to be."

"I don't think so."

"Yes, you could."

"No, I couldn't."

"The part of you I love is very simple."

"The part of me you love is mostly in your head."

"It's in our sex."

"Sex isn't love."

"Wanta bet?"

Uncle Markus is coming to town. "There's a dinner theatre I want to look at," he tells me over the phone. "It's in a place called Mississauga. Do you know it?"

"Yeah. What's the show?"

"Annette Funicello in *Worn-Out Rosie*. Supposedly, it's the best thing she's done since the Mouseketeers."

"Can you get an extra ticket?"

"You want to go?"

"I'd love to go."

"All right," says Uncle Markus. "I'll give you a call after I arrive."

The minute I hang up I get what seems to me a brilliant idea: to fix Uncle Markus up with Snookums. I am not thinking of Uncle Markus. Oh, no. I am thinking purely of Snookums. How he loves husband-shopping more than anything. And what better catch could there possibly be than my uncle?

I plan to plead a previous engagement and send Snookums in my place. And, as luck would have it, I do have a previous engagement. Randy is getting out of the hospital!

On her five o'clock rounds, Dr. Susan Fieldstone pronouces him fit as a fiddle, says there's no need for him to stay until morning, and he might as well go home and get used to sleeping in his own bed.

But when I get to the hospital to pick him up, Randy is in an unusually difficult mood. He thinks it's Christmas.

"Tell me a Christmas story," he says.

"Randy, it's not Christmas. It's August."

"Then tell me a Christmas-in-August story."

"You're being very difficult."

"I want my story."

"Look, it's hot outside. People are wearing shorts. There's no snow."

"Still, it smells like Christmas."

"That's because you're eating an orange."

He turns toward the window. There's a ledge you can sit on. It's cluttered with old flowers and newspapers. He wriggles in amid the mess and looks out at the grounds. At the sidewalk. At the people coming and going. He presses his hand to the glass like a character in a TV movie.

"I thought I'd never get out of here," he says. "Not that I cared. I just wanted it to be all over with, you know? But I feel very differently now. Better than I've felt in years, Zero. And I want a story to go with it."

"OK," I concede. "You'll get your story."

"It was Christmas Eve," I begin. "I was ten years old. My semiretarded cousin and I had this ritual of dressing our great-grandmother up, sort of like a pageant. Great-Grandmother loved it. Loved the attention. And the costumes. It was the only time anybody ever looked at her. She spent most of her life locked in the attic. She only got out to use the bathroom and to sit on the porch every afternoon, where she presided over our street, applauding the neighbors she approved of and spitting on those she didn't.

"Hortense, Granddaddy, Mom, Dad, Norm, Doll, Aunt Lydia, Stellrita, and Trombone were all down in the parlor, drinking eggnog, waiting for the Grand Entrance. Trebreh, Great-Grandmother, and I were on the second floor landing putting on the finishing touches.

"We had gone all out that year. We had Great-Grand-mother fixed up just like a Christmas tree. We hooked ornaments on her shawl, dripped icicles over her arm, and had strings of lights wired up and down her body, which lit up by a complicated series of extension cords. The crowning glory was a headband Trebreh had made from masking tape and some sparklers he'd saved over from the Fourth of July. He fixed it so the sparklers stood straight up, like the crown on the Statue of Liberty.

"Great-Grandmother was ecstatic. She actually teared up when she saw herself in the mirror. Then Treb and I began lighting the sparklers. It as an incredible sight. As the sparks flitted about her head and she began her descent, she said, 'Boys, you've pleased me beyond all expectation! Why, I could die in this moment a happy woman.'

"A hush fell over even the most cynical members of the family as Great-Grandmother glided into view. She looked so regal, so sophisticated, so much like—well, a Christmas tree.

"Then, out of nowhere, her head burst into a huge fireball. The doctor said later it must have been something in her hairspray that ignited when the sparklers burned down. And before we knew it, the flames spread to her clothes.

Mom and Hortense started dousing her with eggnog, which only made her scream all the louder and did nothing to quell the flames. Finally Dad tackled her on a throw rug and rolled her up in it. Then Stellrita went and called an ambulance.

"By the time the fire was out, Great-Grandmother hadn't a hair left on her head. As for the rest of her body, we couldn't tell. The ambulance people just picked her up wrapped in the throw rug and carried her away.

"It took hours for the doctors to remove all the shards embedded in her delicate skin from the broken ornaments and Christmas tree lights. We visited her the next day, Christmas. Took her her presents. Took her a cold plate of Christmas dinner, which she refused to eat and would have thrown at us had the nurse not restrained her. She later threatened to charge Trebreh and me with attempted murder. That scared the hell out of us, though Hortense said not to worry, that Great-Grandmother was just a crazy old woman and no one'd listen to her anyway. After all, she had voluntarily let us use those sparklers when she should have known full well what might have happened.

"Her hair never grew back. And she refused to wear wigs, on principle, though we gave her one on every possible present-giving occasion.

"I'll never forget the day she got out of the hospital. It was shortly after New Year's. She insisted on walking home, and god knows why, but Hortense let her. Not that it was far. It wasn't. Just a few blocks. But Great-Grandmother walked right down Main Street in her nightgown and slippers. She had a little pink bow Scotch-taped to her scalp and a sign around her neck, which she wore for the rest of her life, that said LOOK WHAT THEY DID TO ME."

Randy laughs, as he's supposed to, and gives me an energetic hug. "That's a great story, but it can't possibly be true."

"It's true enough." I throw my arm over his shoulder, then kiss him smack dab on the lips. "Come on, honey. I'm takin' you home!"

Dear Lance,

Randy and I are housecleaning. His place is such a pigsty I've had to send him down to the store for some more Comet. Anyway, I've been meaning to write and apologize for leaving so abruptly that night at Discovery, but simply haven't had the time to give it the attention you deserve. But believe me, Lance, meeting you was the saving grace of my Little Rock trip and I want you to know it.

Uncle Markus has been in town. For some perverse and illogical reason I tried to fix him up with Snookums, an older friend of mine. Never, in your wildest dreams, attempt such a thing.

They went, as you might imagine, to a dinner theatre. Snookums, in his nervousness, drank himself silly. He embarrassed Uncle Markus terribly in front of his business associates, going on and on about love and marriage. And if that wasn't enough, he tripped and fell on the way out. And no simple fall this. Oh, no. He fell into Uncle Markus, who in turn lost his balance and fell into the man from the dinner theatre. Then they all went tumbling over a hedge and into the parking lot. Splat!

Snookums, fortunately, was lubricated enough to escape without a bruise. The man from the dinner theatre only tore his trousers and lost the skin off his knees. But poor Uncle Markus suffered compound fractures in both legs. So he went into the hospital the day Randy came out!

My letter is interrupted by the jiggling of keys at the apartment door.

"What took you so long?" I ask.

But when the door opens, I see that it's not Randy. It's Jesus Las Vegas. And with three suitcases . . . .

"What are *you* doing here?"

"It's where I live, remember?"

"I thought you were stayin' in the South."

"That was just my vacation."

"You mean Searce didn't call you?"

"Call me about what?"

"Show Babies has been shut down. The whole block is

in the process of being razed. He and his army of drag queens are at the mayor's office right now with their daily demonstration. You oughta go down and help 'em."

"Poor Searce!" says Jesus, making a hasty retreat to the guest room to change into Judy Garland. "How's Randy?" he asks.

"Great!"

"Where is he?"

"Loblaw's. Apparently having the time of his life. He's been gone over an hour."

"What's all this stuff in my room?"

"It's mine. I've been stayin' over."

"Problems with Clay?"

"No. I hate to disappoint you, but I just wanted to be here for Randy."

"Why should that disappoint me?"

Judy emerges looking splendid. He stops to adjust his pantyhose. "Where exactly is the mayor's office?"

"City Hall. Any cab driver can get you there. And Jesus—"

"Yeah?"

"I don't think it's a good idea for you to plan on stayin' here."

"Why? I can look after Randy and you can go home."

"No, that's not how it's gonna be. You're gonna check into the Selby Hotel, and if you don't have the money, I'll loan it to you."

He looks at me quizzically. "Sure. Whatever you say."

Randy does not come home until after midnight. I consider calling the Bureau of Missing Persons, but having a general distaste for authority, decide against it. Instead, I just worry myself sick and eventually fall asleep on the couch.

The instant I hear his key in the lock, I jump awake.

He is not alone. Following behind him is a hunky blond who smiles and introduces himself as Alan.

Randy hands me the bag with the Comet. He and Alan are holding hands. "We met in Loblaw's checkout line," he says dreamily.

"Where have you been?"

"Everywhere."

"Why didn't you call?"

"It never entered my mind."

With a wink, he leads Alan to the bedroom.

A moment later Randy reappears. "Forgot something," he says and reaches in the bag. He pulls out a tube of K-Y and a fresh pack of rainbow condoms.

I can't get back to sleep for the life of me. Or for the sounds of them fucking—on and on and on. You'd think they'd just invented it! Finally, I take one of Randy's sleeping pills and am dead to the world until eleven the next morning.

I find Randy out on the balcony drinking a pot of coffee. There's no sign of Alan.

"I've finally met him," he says.

"Who?" I ask, pouring myself a cup.

"The love of my life."

"You can't know that in one night."

"Yes, you can. You knew it with David. And with Clay."

"And look where I am now."

"I will not bear your cynicism, Zero. Not on this day of most perfect days. If you can't say something joyous, say nothing at all." He leans back in his chair, gripping the balcony rail with his toes. "Guess what else?"

"I can't imagine."

"Alan works in film. He's the art director for my movie."

"I *don't* believe it!"

"You've been a sweetheart to stay with me. But I don't think it'll be necessary any longer."

"Why not?" I ask defensively.

"I've asked Alan to move in."

"A clear sign of dementia!"

"Not dementia, dear. I've never felt more sure of anything in my life. He's just in town for the film. And it's already arranged. He'll be here with his stuff by dinnertime. I hope you can stay and eat with us. I'd really like you to get to know him."

"Sure."

"Great."

"May I ask you a personal question?"

"Go ahead, you'll ask anyway."

"Does he know you've been sick?"

"Yes. I told him all about it."

"And?"

"He's an asymptomatic seropositive and part of a big study in Vancouver. He's on all the same medication I am. Is that not remarkable?"

"Like the kind of thing that only happens in movies." I sink into a chair. "So why don't I feel happy for you, Randy? Why do I feel like I've just lost my left arm?"

That night's dinner party consists of me, Randy, Jesus Las Vegas, and Alan (who even cooks).

Jesus is down in the guest room packing, having spent the previous night with someone he picked up at the demonstration.

Randy talks excitedly about the film. "It's by far the best part I've ever had. I know it's bad luck to say so, but I've got a feeling about this project, a feeling it could be one of the best Canadian films ever made."

Alan smiles through the pass-through. "It's true."

"Is this guy too much, or what?" says Randy.

"Too much," I mumble. Then: "Here's to winning the Genie for Best Actor." I raise my glass in a toast.

"Fuck the Genie!" says Randy. "All I care about is that you're by my side at the premiere."

"What about your new love interest?" I whisper.

"I have two sides," he reminds me. "I wouldn't have made it through this year without you, Zero."

"Yes, you would've."

"Still, you're the one who sent me down to Loblaw's for Comet."

"Biggest mistake of my life."

"Dinner's ready," announces Alan.

"What'd you make?" I ask.

"Spinach crepes."

"Oh," I reply. "The simple menu."

After we eat, I am dying to get out of there and offer to help Jesus carry his bags to the Selby.

I wait for him while he checks in, then help him carry them up to the room.

I sit on the lumpy bed, feeling strangely unmotivated. I watch him unpack his dresses and carefully hang them in the closet. His jeans and T-shirts just stay stacked in a heap.

He sits down beside me. It feels good being there with him, and I tell him so.

"You're a good friend to people, Zero."

"Am I?" I wonder.

"One of the best I've seen."

"I haven't been very good to you."

"Yes, you have."

I say nothing.

"Why don't we do something fun tonight?" says Jesus. "Like go to a movie."

"I'd love to go to a movie, but I can't. I've gotta go by the hospital and check on my uncle. He's in traction, you know."

"Want me to come along?"

"No. Uncle Markus wouldn't like it, and you'd just have to wait in the hall."

"Well, it beats sitting around here."

I still haven't forgiven you," says Uncle Markus, "so don't expect me to be nice."

"I don't," I say humbly.

"I just can't fathom what sort of madness could have provoked you to set me up on a date."

"I wanted you to have some fun. I don't want you to be lonely."

"I'm not lonely! And to think I'd even be interested in such a man."

"Snookums is very dear to me, Uncle Markus. Once you get to know him—"

"Get to know him? Even if I liked him I make it a point never to socialize with people who wear hairpieces."

"He can't help it if he's bald."

"He should be proud to be bald! That damn hairpiece fell off when we went tumbling into the parking lot, and he looks much better without it. Almost . . . considerable."

"I'll tell him you said so."

"Don't you tell him any such thing!"

"All right! For what it's worth, I promise never to fix you up again. The next time you come to town it'll just be you and me."

"The next time?"

"You have my word, Uncle Markus."

"What I have is two broken legs! You ought to see my X-rays. There're more squiggles in my bones than in a map of the Mississippi delta. And to think about even visiting you again. I don't know if I'll ever get out of this hellhole, much less have the chance to return!"

"Uncle Markus, it's not good for you to get too excited."

"I am not the least bit excited! The doctor tells me I'll be in traction another four weeks and have casts on my legs for six months. Do you think that's anything to get excited about? How am I supposed to get around? How am I supposed to run my business?"

"You'll just have to get a nurse. And a wheelchair. Accidents happen—"

"What kind of a nurse? I'm seventy-two years old. I do not intend to spend six months being bullied by some hard-nosed crank!"

"All nurses are not cranks, for chrissake."

"What I need is a companion. A *male* companion. Someone who shares my sensibilities. Someone with charm. Someone who knows how to open a decent bottle of champagne. I need my Jack!" he cries.

Suddenly I get an idea.

"Excuse me a minute, Uncle Markus." I run out in the hall to where Jesus is sitting and join him. "I know you must be worried about being unemployed," I say.

"No, not really—"

"Well, you should be."

"Why? Since when did worrying do any good?"

"Since five minutes ago, because I have a job for you."

"What kind of job?"

"Working for my uncle."

"In one of his dinner theatres?" asks Jesus excitedly.

"Maybe after you get to know him. But what he needs right now is a companion."

"Contrary to what you think, Zero MacNoo, I'm an entertainer, not a whore."

"Believe me, those skills will prove vital in this assignment. Uncle Markus is a rich man. You'll be paid well. It'll give you a chance to befriend him. Get on his good side. And I'm sure a part in one of his productions will certainly follow."

"I don't know, Zero. I've always wanted to go legit, but this seems like a pretty roundabout way of doin' it."

"Then think of the money! That alone oughta be enough to tempt you."

I watch the wheels begin to turn in his pretty little head. Jesus stops one of the nurses and asks what he'd be paid for private duty. His eyes pop at the amount.

I take that as my cue to lead him into my uncle's room.

"Uncle Markus, I'd like you to meet Jesus Las Vegas. He's willing to be your companion. He knows how to open a bottle of champagne. He shares your sensibilities. And he could charm the pants off Rambo if necessary."

Uncle Markus' eyes only betray a slight hint of interest. "Have you any experience?" he asks.

"Yes," pipes Jesus. "I worked as a candy striper all through high school."

"How much do you charge?"

"The going rate. A thousand a week plus expenses. A registered nurse would cost twice that."

Uncle Markus gags.

"What I suggest," I offer, "is a trip. It'd give you a chance to relax. And it's a well-known fact the healing process happens much quicker when you're enjoying yourself."

"Where could I possibly go in this condition?" Uncle Markus says indignantly. "And what about my business?"

"Oh, your business practically runs itself. You've already booked *Worn-Out Rosie*. Surely your managers can handle the rest. And I'm not suggesting you climb the Himalayas. Do something like a cruise. All you'd have to do is sit there, soak up the sun, take the air, and be waited on."

"But there's no place I want to go I haven't already been."

"What about the Greek islands? You've never been there, and they look great from a boat."

"I'd love to see Greece!" squeals Jesus. "If you take me to Greece I'll do it for seven hundred a week!"

Jesus strikes a charming pose accompanied by an irresistible smile.

Uncle Markus picks up the phone with a stern look. For a moment I fear he's calling security to have us thrown out.

"Give me the number of a travel agent," he says to the operator. "I don't care how much you charge for information. Goddammit, I want that number!"

Searcy and I sit at Fran's drinking coffee. His army of drag queens has dwindled to a precious few. The politics of the situation seems to have lost its momentum.

"Being a drag queen," he explains, "is, in and of itself, a political act. Somewhere between hair spray and hemlines, the girls have found more pressing things to do with their lunch hours than help our little cause. Not that I blame them."

I'm supposed to be here cheering him up. But depression is contagious among friends. So we just look at each other, jittering on a caffeine high, as the waitresses slug their way from one table to the next.

Prompted by my diminishing bank balance, I make an appointment to have that business talk with Snookums. I meet him down at the office.

"How's your uncle?" he asks.

"Another two weeks of traction."

"I feel just terrible about the whole thing. Do you think he'd mind if I went by to see him?"

"I think he'd probably kill you."

"Well, I sent some flowers—"

"Let's just hope he doesn't read the card."

Snookums leads me toward Maurice's office.

"Wait a minute. I came to meet with you, not Maurice."

"I told you there had been some changes, and this is one of them. The editorial board finally ousted the son of a bitch. And guess who's acting editor in chief while the Search Committee searches? Queen Snookums! Now do you think you'd be interested in writing for us?"

"Writing what?"

"A column. Stories about Toronto. About the people you know, the things you've seen."

"Oh, Snookums—" The very thought of being needed again makes me burst into tears.

"What in heaven's name is the matter, precious?"

"I don't know!" I wail. "PMS. I've finally lost my grip."

"Then I'm taking you up to Robert's for some lunch and a little heart-to-heart talk."

I bawl the whole way there. Snookums shields me from the passersby with a file folder.

He leads me to the restaurant section at the back of the bar, telling the waiter, "Get this girlie a double anything. And make it snappy!"

The waiter brings me a huge martini, which I sip between sobs.

Snookums listens patiently to my complaints, full of the empathy and understanding of a doting auntie.

"Then to top it all, this thing with Randy and Alan . . . I know it's crazy, but I feel so betrayed. It's like I've lost him. He doesn't need me anymore. Not like he did. Anytime I see him, it's with Alan. Anytime I try to plan anything, he has to check with Alan. Alan's taken my place!"

"No, he hasn't, precious. No one could take your place. They're just in love."

"Love!" I sneer. "What is love but some compromise between two people's individuality so they can ignore the fact that we all end up alone? The real eye-opener is the love between friends. I thought that was different. I thought that was the one thing that lasts forever."

"How do you know it doesn't? Why don't you just wait and see?"

"Because I'm sick and tired of waiting! I've spent my whole life waiting. And for what? I used to want to feel everything, Snookums, to the point of bursting. Now all I want is to feel nothing."

"Don't you think you're getting a little carried away? One advantage of having Alan with Randy is that it leaves you free to move to condoland with Clay."

I sob anew. "No. I haven't told anyone this yet, but I've decided not to move to that condo."

"You haven't even told Clay?"

"I'm telling him tonight."

"Oh, my goodness gracious, you don't mean to say you're leaving him?"

"I'd say it was more like he was leaving me. He's the one who bought the damn thing."

"Then where do you plan to live? There's no vacancy in this city. And even if you can find a place, the rent's so high who can afford it?"

"I don't know." The idea of being homeless brings a fresh flood of tears. "I hadn't thought of that."

"There, there, precious. Don't fret."

"How can I not fret?"

"Because . . . I happen to know of a lovely place for rent."

"You do?"

"Yes. On the second floor of an old house. Three big rooms. And it's only four hundred a month."

"Sounds like a miracle."

"It just may be." He hands me his hankie. "Here. You dry your eyes. I'm gonna run downstairs and call to make sure it's still available."

I mop my tears. Down the rest of my martini.

A few minutes later, Snookums reappears.

"It's still available, and the landlord's on his way here to meet you right now!"

David walks by on the sidewalk looking cool and collected. He turns into Robert's. Great! Just what I need, an ex-lover to gloat as my life falls apart. I pray he doesn't see us, but no such luck. He spots us right off, waves, and heads straight for our table.

"So where's my new tenant?" he asks.

As soon as I realize what Snookums has done, I want to crown him. But he beats such a hasty retreat I don't have a chance. "I believe my presence," he says, "to be redundant at this point."

"Would you mind explaining to me what's going on?" asks David.

I throw my hands up in the air, all caution to the wind, and just tell him the whole shebang.

He listens intently, then says, "Fine. The people who rent my second floor are leaving at the end of the month. I'd love for you to have it."

"You would?"

"Sure. Why not? We're friends, aren't we? And I know you're a conscientious tenant. Besides, it's against the law, Zero, to discriminate. Even against ex-lovers."

I'm smiling again. I feel like getting down on my knees and kissing his suntanned feet.

On my way back to Clay's I run into Searcy.

"Zero, guess what I've just endured."

"Can't imagine."

"An audition, god forbid."

"What for?"

"Les Cavaliers needs a piano player. To lead the cocktail hour sing-along. The ultimate in humiliation, but I suppose it beats Fran's."

"Great, Searce. I'd love to hear all about it, but I've gotta run."

"Where are you off to in such a hurry?"

"I'm late getting groceries. I've gotta make a nice dinner for Clay."

"What have you done now?"

"You'll hear about it soon enough!"

I put potatoes in the oven to bake. Make a Caesar salad. Salt and pepper a couple of filets, which I'll pan-fry rare right before we eat.

While Clay's at the gym, I root through the moving boxes

he's already packed and fill one suitcase with my most prized possessions. I hide it in the storage closet down by the elevators just in case.

I'm sitting on the couch flipping through a magazine when he gets in.

I immediately fix him a drink and suggest he slip into something more comfortable. "Like maybe your jockstrap."

He complies right on the spot, a sexy smile on his face.

I follow him into the bedroom for what I fear may be our last good time.

As we sit down to dinner, I make my big announcement. It doesn't seem to faze him at first. He just keeps on buttering his potato, then asks very calmly where I'm gonna live.

I tell him.

That's when I get the fit I expected.

"Of all possible places, why, why, *why* would you have to pick David's?"

"I didn't pick it. He had a vacancy. It's a nice place and a good deal. The fact that it's in David's house is purely coincidental."

"Nothing in this world is coincidental."

"Everything in this world is coincidental!"

"And just where does that leave us?"

"Lovers, I hope. We just won't be living together."

He laughs. It's a mean laugh. A laugh I haven't heard from him before.

"What kind of lovers? Lovers who just get together to screw? Well, I happen to need someone who needs a little more from me than my cock."

"Clay, look at us. Look at how different we are. What have we got in common? You don't like my friends. You're not interested in my work."

"And you're so interested in mine?"

"No. I'm not. And if you want to get married so badly, why don't you go find yourself a Simpson's clerk? There're a million people out there who'd be thrilled to move into that condo with you, and who you'd find much more compatible than me."

Clay actually begins to cry.

I am astonished. "Clay, please—"

"I thought there was more between us than this."

"There is. People would die for what we have."

"I invested something in you, Zero. Something you took for granted. Something you never even realized. I thought we'd last. I thought of all the people I'd been through, you were the one."

"I just don't want to move into that condo, Clay. Don't make it more than it is."

"But I bought it for *us!*"

"No, you didn't. But that's not the point. You *should* have the condo. It's just not for me."

"Then what is?"

"Snookums offered me a job today. Writing."

"That's not what I asked."

I look at my plate. I haven't taken one bite. "I want to live alone, Clay."

"Alone with David."

"The second floor of David's house is a separate apartment unto itself."

"Still, you'll see him all the time."

"So what? We're friends."

"You'll have dinner with him—"

"Not if I'm having dinner with you."

"Well, you won't be, so you needn't worry about that. In fact, you won't be seeing me at all."

"Don't you think that's being a little childish?"

"Get out."

"I find it hard to believe all our passion could end like this."

"I said get out."

"Won't you miss it?"

"I'll miss the person you never could be."

And to that, I have no reply. All I feel is shame. Then

fury. I'd like to hit him and feel him hit me back. I'd like something concrete, but I don't get it. I just take him at his word and walk out.

As I retrieve my suitcase from the storage closet, I hear an entire table full of dishes go crashing to the floor.

The sound cuts through my heart.

Like love.

I end up staying at the Selby Hotel until my apartment's ready. Several people offer to put me up, but I meant what I said about being on my own. I've even resumed work on one of my plays.

In no time at all it seems I'm writing David a check for my second month's rent, and Randy and Alan are leaving for Vancouver. Searcy offers to drive them to the airport. I go along as well.

Searce sends me up to the apartment to see if they need any help. Randy sits, bag in hand, by the front door as Alan dashes about, fresh from the shower, frantically throwing things into a suitcase.

"It's when you take your first trip together," Randy comments, "that you really start to get to know each other."

"Well, he'd better hurry. Searcy's parked in the fire lane."

"Alan, come on!"

"I'm coming!"

"Want me to carry anything down?" I ask.

"No, I've just got the one bag."

"For two months?"

"Yeah. Few pairs of jeans, few T-shirts, few sweaters, my leather jacket. What more does a movie star need?"

"I can think of a million things, from autograph seekers to acceptance speeches."

"Want to be my new agent?"

"Sure." I laugh.

Alan joins us, tousled and bothered and tucking in his shirttail. "Well," he says breathlessly, "I guess I'm ready."

"About time," says Randy, ushering us into the hallway. Carefully, he locks the apartment door.

Once we're in the elevator, he says, "Oh god, I wonder if I remembered to empty the garbage."

"Yes," says Alan. "You also remembered to turn off the stove."

"He's like this every time he leaves home," I say. "Randy thinks his apartment is gonna self-destruct in his absence."

"You do the same thing, Zero."

"I'm not as bad about it as you are."

We step off the elevator and walk out to the car. Searcy is having a very animated conversation with himself.

"What are you on about?" I ask.

"Trying to see if I know all the words to 'Send in the Clowns.' It's my new theme song."

"How apropos," says Randy, tossing his bag into the trunk.

"That's right, kick me when I'm down."

"Sure is nice of you to come pick us up," says Alan.

"Oh, it's my pleasure. I love going out to the airport. It's such a good place to meet people. People who travel! And I'd do anything for you, Alan. Anything in the world."

Randy and I roll our eyes. "May we go?"

"Certainly," says Searcy. "But, Alan, if you should ever get tired of Randall . . ."

"I know where to find you." Alan laughs, taking Randy's hand.

We make it to the airport in record time. "Seventeen minutes!" exclaims Searce. He lets us off on the departure level. "Where shall I meet you girls?"

"By the newsstand," says Alan. "I need to get myself something to read."

"Okie-doke. Be there as soon as I can find a parking place."

The terminal is packed. Randy and I stand in the check-in line. Oddly enough, we seem to have very little to say to each other. Or maybe so much to say we don't know where to begin.

"Excited?" I finally ask.

"You bet."

"Who would've thought, huh?"

"Not I." He shakes his head. "What a summer."

"No kidding."

"You have the number at Alan's, don't you?"

"I do."

"And the address?"

"I've got it all written down at home."

"Tickets?" asks the counter clerk. Randy hands them over. She taps their names into the computer.

"A window and a middle," says Randy. "And toward the front, if you've got it."

I help him hoist the bags onto the weigh scale. The counter clerk tags them and puts them on the conveyor belt. The computer spits out the boarding passes. "There you go." She smiles. "Gate seventy-two. Have a nice flight."

At the newsstand, a group of religious fundamentalists are trying to solicit support for their war on drugs, abortion, and homosexuality. Searcy takes their pamphlet, crams it in his mouth, chews it several times, then spits it out.

"You won't change those types," Randy says. "Why even waste your energy?"

"For the sheer joy of it! It just makes me furious that they can wander around the airport handing out hate literature. There ought to be a law."

"There is. It's called freedom of speech. So try to get a grip on it, will you?"

We troop down the corridor to the security checkpoint. That's where we say our goodbyes.

Alan and I shake hands warmly.

"Take care of each other," I tell him.

"You can be sure we will."

"Think Garbo!" says Searce.

Randy and I hug hard. Then he holds me at arm's length. "I expect you to come out and visit me next month."

"I'll be there."

"Let me know how much your ticket is. I'll gladly pay half."

"You don't have to do that."

"I insist."

"In that case—"

"You'll love Vancouver, Zero."

"I love you."

"I love you too."

We hug once more, grinning like fools.

"Good luck with the movie," I say.

"Good luck with the column."

"Now get out of here before you miss your plane."

Randy sets off the metal detector. The security guard has him empty his pockets and try again. He still sets it off. As the guard runs the sensor rod up between his legs, Randy throws us one last mug.

I slip my arm through Searcy's, and, with a sweet sort of melancholy, we stroll to the car.

The ride back to town is a quiet one. But when we pull off the expressway smack dab into rush-hour traffic, Searcy starts glancing nervously at his Lady Timex. "Shit bricks. At this rate I'll be late for Les Cavaliers."

"What time do you have to be there?"

"Five. And . . . I'm on probation."

"What for?"

"All those queens ever want me to play are the 'M' songs. You know: 'Misty,' 'Mammy,' 'Memory.' I get so sick of it. Yesterday, I went berserk. Played 'Rose's Turn' over and over again until the whole place emptied out. Management was not amused. It's just that I miss performing, Zero. Piano bars don't really count. I miss my gowns, my spotlight."

"Oh, you'll be back onstage in no time."

"I'd like to know where," he says, an edge of desperation in his voice.

"You'll just have to take over another club."

"Is that all?"

"Listen, if you're running late, why don't you let me off at the next corner?"

"Sure you don't mind?"

"Nope. The walk'll do me good."

He pulls over at the bus stop. "You're a lifesaver, Zero."

"Thanks for driving us."

"No problem."

"Talk to you soon."

" 'Bye, hon."

" 'Bye."

I head up Church Street to David's.

I lose people.

Sometimes they come back; sometimes not.

About the Author

Peter McGehee is the author of two collections of stories, *Beyond Happiness* and *The I. Q. Zoo*. He wrote the songs for and performed in the musical revues *The Quinlan Sisters* and *The Fabulous Sirs*, both of which toured Canada extensively and played on the CBC. Originally from Arkansas, he has lived in Dallas, San Francisco, Saskatoon, New York, and, currently, Toronto. *Boys Like Us* is his first novel.

Lizards Don't Wear Lip Gloss

by Trina Wiebe

Illustrations
by Marisol Sarrazin

Lobster Press ™

To my parents, Larry and Teresa Fletcher,
for their love and support. Happy Anniversary!

Lizards Don't Wear Lip Gloss
Text copyright © 2000 by Trina Wiebe
Illustrations copyright © 2000 by Marisol Sarrazin

Published in 2005 by Lobster Press™
1620 Sherbrooke St. West, Suites C & D
Montréal, Québec H3H 1C9
Tel. (514) 904-1100 • Fax (514) 904-1101
www.lobsterpress.com • www.abbyandtess.com

Publisher: Alison Fripp
Editor: Jane Pavanel
Cover design: Marielle Maheu
Inside design: Geneviève Mayers
Production Manager: Tammy Desnoyers

We acknowledge the financial support of the Government of Canada
through the Book Publishing Industry Development Program (BPIDP)
for our publishing activities.

The Canada Council | Le Conseil des Arts
for the Arts | du Canada

We acknowledge the support of
the Canada Council for the Arts
for our publishing program.

Canadian Cataloguing in Publication Data
Wiebe, Trina, 1970-
ISBN 1-894222-11-3

I. Sarrazin, Marisol, 1965- II. Title. III. Series: Wiebe, Trina, 1970-
Abby and Tess, Pet-Sitters.

PS8595.I358L59 2000   jC813'.6   C00-900449-1
PZ7.W6349Li2000

Printed and bound in Canada

Contents